T0162002

A MAN WHO IS
NOT A MAN

A MAN WHO IS
NOT A MAN

Thando Mgqolozana

CASSAVA REPUBLIC

Abuja – London

First published in 2020 by Cassava Republic Press
Abuja – London

Copyright © Thando Mgqolozana

All rights reserved. No part of this book may be reproduced, stored in a retrieval system, or transported in any form or by any means (electronic, mechanical, photocopying, recording or otherwise), without the prior written permission of the publisher of this book.

The moral right of Thando Mgqolozana to be identified as the Author of this work has been asserted by him in accordance with the Copyright, Designs and Patents Act 1988.

This is a work of fiction. Names, characters, businesses, places and incidents are either the product of the author's imagination or are used fictitiously. Any resemblance to actual persons, living or dead, events or locales is entirely coincidental.

A CIP catalogue record for this book is available from the National Library of Nigeria and British Library.

ISBN 9781913175023
eISBN 9781913175030

Book design by AI's Fingers
Cover Design by Alex Kirby

Printed and bound in Great Britain by Bell and Bain Ltd., Glasgow

Distributed in Nigeria by Yellow Danfo
Distributed in the UK by Central Books Ltd.
Distributed in the US by Consortium Books

Stay up to date with the latest books, special offers and exclusive content with our monthly newsletter.

Sign up on our website:
www.cassavarepublic.biz

Twitter: @cassavarepublic
Instagram: @cassavarepublicpress
Facebook: facebook.com/CassavaRepublic
Hashtag: #AManWho #ReadCassava

This story is about how I came to have an abnormal penis. So, there you have it: my genitalia is not the normal type. By that I mean it hasn't got the distinctive lollipop shape with a knobbly head that most men boast of.

Let me say that's not because I was born this way. When I was a boy, the potential and everything was there, you know. There are no funny stories related about me at birth. Some boys get told that their willies were so small their mothers gave them girls' names. Me, I was a real boy from the get-go, with both my balls fully descended and the promising look that I would one day own a formidable loin. But Satan had other plans.

Have you ever wondered what happens to *abakhwetha* whose circumcision fails at the bush? You have seen their sorrowful white-smeared faces and bulgy bloodshot eyes. You have seen their ugly shaven heads weighed down with shame and disappointment. I'm talking about the young Xhosa boys whose misfortune affords them the costly opportunity to grab news headlines.

If you belong to the zero point zero zero one per cent of South Africans who have not heard about or seen these boys, I suggest you consult your nearest media house. The Eastern Cape's *Daily Dispatch* must hold the record for such stories on its archived front pages. Call up the newspaper first thing tomorrow and write your thesis on it.

You may want to formulate your hypothesis according to the following questions: Who exactly are these miscreants whose circumcision fails? What type of people were they before they were circumcised? What happens to them at the mountain? And who do they become afterwards? That's an important one: who do they become.

Well, you might not need to call up that newspaper anymore, because here I am. I'm one of those survivors! And this is what I have become: a survivor, not a victim. Victims are the lot who didn't make it through to lunch. They are the ones who just give up on life after their tragedy. Some die from septicaemia and dehydration, some decide to quit life, literally. Others live on but resign themselves to a lifetime of shame and ridicule, surrendering to the traditional penalties demanded by other men whenever they are found out. I used to think that those were the victims. And that I and others like me, who choose to disappear mysteriously into society after our ordeal, were the survivors. But I was wrong. I've come to understand that living in fear of being found out, constantly having to hide what I am, is not the survival I want.

That word "survivor" is an interesting one. It means a lot more than simply resolving not to commit suicide or being able to put up with the social exclusion. It involves more than pretending I have defeated my pain while I'm still hurting from it. Or clinging to the eternal hope that one day I will be rescued from my misery by some external force and remade into a man the right way, so I can live happily ever after with my deformed penis.

You see, survival starts from within, like a pregnancy, a tiny seed that gradually grows stronger, expanding day by day. As a so-called failed man, I have had to gain a new understanding of myself in context. I no longer look at my world in the same way, through the world's eyes; a recipe for discrimination, that! I have had to learn to look through my eyes, and then adjust the world's view of the way it looks at me. But to do that, I first had to accept and love who I have become. That hasn't been quick or easy. It has taken me a long time to understand that I don't have to live by the conditioning of my society, which determines my acceptance into it or otherwise. My self-image is no longer dependent on what my society thinks of me but what I think of it.

Writing this story is my way of bringing finality to that process. I'm laying the ghosts to rest, so to speak. I would like to think that I am neither stuck in one village called Victimhood, where there are pitiable moans, nor in the neighbouring one called Victimville, where "what ifs" punctuate every sentence. If you want to reach me, I can be found at Survivorville, down Hope Street, at Self-acceptance City.

1

Waking up into the sudden brightness of that room hurt my eyes. I used my hand to cover my glued eyelids and wipe the sleep off them. The fluorescence was so bright it penetrated my palms. I rubbed my eyelids with my fists, hoping to unglue them and regain my sight; I could not. There was this vast heaviness that would not allow my eyelids to lift, as if the brightness had welded them shut. A soft and gentle voice called my name. It reminded me of the comforting voice of my first grade teacher. I struggled some more with my eyelids and suddenly, they flipped open. God must have had a reason to keep them shut for so long because when they finally did open, I woke up to a world of sorrow.

'Is something the matter, *mfana*?' asked the first-grade-teacher voice that had earlier intruded on my sleep. I had been dreaming about the five remaining stones at my hut. I looked in the direction of the voice, which was coming from above me, and saw not the weathered visage of my teacher, but the smooth and beautiful face of an angel. The face belonged to a nurse in a white uniform with maroon epaulettes. She had a gold necklace draped around her neck and a name badge pinned to her right breast pocket. Her relaxed hair was pushed back from her face and tied into a ponytail at the back.

'Is something the matter, *mfana*? Do you need something?' the nurse asked again, softly. She glanced in the direction of the other patients in the ward, who were asleep, then brought her attention back to me, widening the whites of her eyes.

'No...' I said. I was still a little confused. Maybe I was hoping that all of this was part of the dream I had been having, from which I would suddenly awaken for real. As the seconds ticked away, it became clear that I was not dreaming. I was a patient, admitted to a hospital.

The nurse reached up to check the half-full saline bag hanging over me. She turned it, observing the rhythm of the tiny drops that dripped from it. I realised that the saline bag was inserted into my wrist. I imagined I felt each tiny drop entering my blood vessels and travelling up my arm to my shoulder, where it disappeared.

'Well... I will let you sleep, then.'

She pulled the panic button out from under my pillow and hung it on the wall above my head. Then she patted my bed and walked away towards the mouth of the ward. I watched her as she checked on the other patients. She switched the overhead light off and walked out without looking back.

In my heart, the chest people beat faster and harder as sober reality drifted in. I pulled my pillow up and adjusted it so that I had a full view of the ward. The lights in the corridor provided enough illumination for me to see by. I looked at the window on my right and saw darkness behind the blinds, telling me it was still night-time.

My eyes browsed the ward. There were three beds on each side. Each bed was framed by curtains which could be drawn around the bed when needed. At the bottom of the beds were those adjustable trolley tables, where they put the patient folders. I was in the corner bed on the side furthest from the mouth of the ward. The ward, the beds, the linen — everything was engulfed in whiteness.

I noticed that the two patients on my left had covered their heads with the white hospital blankets. The bed opposite me was vacant, but the two next to it also had patients in them. They were asleep, and the light had not disturbed them. They both lay on their backs, knees drawn up, in the position in which initiates must sit at the mountain, knees up all the time. I realised that the two patients must be in a similar situation to me. At the thought of my own condition, the chest people started to thud faster again. I recalled my arrival here.

It must have been about 8pm when my grandfather and I walked into the lit foyer. I had my white blanket draped around me and my face was still smeared in white clay.

My eyes were bloodshot; I hadn't slept for the past three days and nights. Grandfather was wearing his usual blue overall coat. His hands were clasped behind him, one on top of the other, in the way he holds them when he is angry about something. His lips were shaking and the watery eyes narrowed, as if to avoid seeing what was to happen next. I hung back as we walked into the brightness of the hospital. I was no longer used to the glare of electric light. On the mountain, I had had only a tiny handmade lamp that gave off light no stronger than a candle.

I lagged behind Grandfather as we walked into the waiting area. Dozens of maroon chairs stood vacant on our left. Dozens of wheelchairs were parked against the wall on our right. The distance that we walked was probably no more than 15 metres from the van that had brought us, but I missed my leaning stick even so. In the three days and nights that I had spent on the mountain, I hadn't once stood up straight. If I wasn't sitting then I was kneeling, or standing half-bent, balanced against my stick, inventing tactics to endure the agonising pain. The blanket was giving me problems as well. The only time it had had any real use was when I was first brought to the mountain. Then, I was grateful to be covered in it, since it helped to conceal the amount of pain I was in. At the hut, it had served as my sofa, since we weren't allowed to lie down and sleep. Now it felt cumbersome, draped around me while I was trying to hold myself upright. I gave up on walking

erect and stayed bent over, like a 114-year-old grandfather.
My own grandfather glanced at me with an I-have-a-good-
mind-to-boot-you-in-the-ribs look as he walked towards the
nurse at Enquiries. I sat down on one of the maroon chairs,
resolving to keep my eyes cast down. I was ashamed of my
situation and I wished everybody could understand that I
wasn't there by choice.

'Good evening, *tata*,' said the nurse from across the counter.

'Evening, *mntanam*,' Grandfather replied.

'I can see you have brought the boy.'

'Hmm... yes, *mntanam*. It is like that...'

There was no describing that "hmm" of his. It conveyed
all the anger and defeat he felt at having to hand over his
grandson.

'Alright, *tata*,' the nurse said. I dropped my eyes as soon
as she switched her attention to me. I wasn't ready to answer
questions about what had brought me there. Not in front of
everyone. Especially not Grandfather. No.

There was silence.

I could feel their eyes boring into my head as I looked at
the tiled floor. I wished they would hurry up and do what they
had to so that I could be admitted and placed in an empty
side ward, where I wouldn't have to be seen by people. I did
not want to encounter any more faces. I was not used to faces,
or human smells, or speech, or anything. I was no longer a
person, I was a different kind of being from these people. I
did not belong here with them. I did not belong in any place
with people, especially not women. But there I was, defying
the customs and tradition and destroying the whole culture.

I noticed for the first time that my heels were starting to
crack. They were grey from the ash of the fire. I hid them
under the blanket and glanced at my thumb nail, which
appeared to have gathered something like grey mud under it.
The smoothness of the tiles and their coldness irritated me. I
wasn't used to smooth floors like that. It had been three days

and nights since I had felt anything but earth under my feet. Three days and nights; that's a long time.

Let me tell you, five minutes at the bush is equivalent to 24 hours outside of it. That's about one thousand one hundred and fifty-two hours that I had spent in that hut alone. Things had to be strange. Even to sit on such a thing as a plastic chair felt awkward.

I heard the flip of pages as the nurse wrote down the details that Grandfather was mumbling to her.

'Okay, we are done for now, *tata*. I will call the porter to transport him with a wheelchair to the doctor's room,' the nurse told my grandfather.

'Mmh,' he responded. I know in his mind he bellowed 'Wheelchair?' I didn't dare look up, although I was tempted to. Staring at the floor, I saw a pair of scuffed black boots standing right in front of me. They looked formidable, with their thick soles and steel toes. The legs in them were covered in blue overall trousers. They were my grandfather's boots. Something about the way they stood there made me wish I was invisible. The head people started to ask tricky questions such as: *Why is this man standing so close to us? Is he about to boot us in the ribs?* I readied myself to jump the moment I saw him aiming his legs at me.

'Mister Ugly, your services are needed, sir,' the nurse called out in isiXhosa. I saw my grandfather's boots turn away and move forward a little. What a relief! But the head people told me he could still heel me on the chin. As I was readying myself to be heel-booted, a pair of flat navy pushes shuffled themselves out from behind the counter and went to stand next to Grandfather's boots. The pushes faced the other way, too. The legs on the pushes had stockings on them.

'Mister Ugly, sir, please help this young man to the examination room,' the polite nurse requested. It wasn't long before I saw grey wheels parking next to me. The shoes behind the grey wheels were so black and shiny I could imagine the nurses lining up to use them as a mirror when putting on their lipstick. The legs in the shiny shoes were in navy-coloured trousers. All the shoes in front of me then turned to face my bare feet. I swallowed and raised my head just enough to see above their knees.

'Do you think he can manage to hop onto the chair on his own, *tata*?' enquired the person in shiny black shoes.

'He is not sick... he does not need this thing,' Grandfather said.

'He would not be here if he was not sick, *tata*,' countered the voice from the navy pushes. I settled the debate by gathering up my white blanket and hopping onto the wheelchair. The person in shiny shoes wheeled me into another room with even brighter lights. The hospital smell was more concentrated here. I waited for the other sets of shoes to shuffle into the room along with us, and was surprised when they didn't. The person in the shiny shoes did not give me too much time to cogitate on this. The shiny shoes brought this person up in front of me, very close.

What the hell? I thought.

'What business do you have in this place, *mkhwetha*?' asked the voice belonging to the only shoes in the room. Before I could respond, the brown hands of the shiny-shoed person peeled open my white blanket around the waist area, giving him a full view of my limb. I felt his bulgy eyes survey the state of my limb with murderous scrutiny. As he opened the blanket, I smelt the familiar rotting odour from before. I felt my nausea return.

'Shit! What have you done, *mkhwetha*?' said the voice of the shiny-shoed person as he covered up my waist area again. He must have been offended by the smell, judging by the way he threw the blanket back so quickly. I swallowed as I contemplated an answer to the what-have-you-done question. It was such an accusing question. To be honest, it made me feel guilty, never mind feeling like a decaying dog.

'Uhm... I did not do anything, it just...' I began to say, when the voice of the only person in the room roared at me:

'It can't just be like this. You must have done something. Where is your attendant?' He was full of acrimonious questions.

I hated it.

'I was not allocated one.' I simply told him the truth, but not without hesitation.

'What?' he roared in disbelief. There was silence.

'How long were you up there?' he asked, still accusatory.

'Three days–'

'Just three days,' he said, cutting me off before I could tell him it was actually three days and three nights. The shiny shoes walked my accuser away towards the door restlessly. They came back and stood in the same position that they had been standing in ten hours ago. Yes, it felt like ten hours.

'What business do you have in this place, then?' he asked again. I could not answer. It was such a heavy question. How could I, for the life of me, admit my failure? How do you tell another man that you have come to hospital for help, without implying that you have failed to be a man the supposed way?

At that point, a pair of brown leather shoes strode in from the adjoining room. The legs above the brown shoes were in khaki trousers. The outside door opened and, to my relief, the shiny shoes left the room. What a session it had been!

'Hey, buddy. I'm Doctor...' The new voice mentioned the name of the person to whom the brown shoes belonged. A very pale hand appeared, offering a handshake. I was relieved to see its paleness. The cultural barrier between the owner of that hand and I served as a source of mental and emotional security. I was tempted to hold the hand. Except, at that time I wasn't shaking hands with humans. The pale hand obviously didn't know that.

The pale hand's owner took a three-hour walk away from me towards the small wheels at the other end of this very bright room. I heard the rustling of papers.

There was a three-hour silence.

For the first time in two thousand hours, I lifted my head up. The lifting of my head coincided with the opening of the door. A beautiful nurse walked in.

'How are we doing?' The soft and gentle voice of my first-grade teacher had returned.

'Uhm...' I replied. I nodded my head, not knowing how I could describe the way I was doing.

'What have we here?' the nurse asked no one in particular.

She helped herself to my blanket, peeling it open and shooting her eyes at what was inside.

'Mmh,' she said.

That's what she said: 'Mmh'. Then she took about eighty-nine minutes before she added: 'You see, you took too long to come here, *bhuti.*'

She went to the doctor and they both put gloves on while they conspired. I heard something about "gangrene", "speedy surgery" and "possible amputation". Yes, those things.

The nurse came back to me, holding giant silver scissors big enough to qualify as a makeshift lawn mower. She used them to cut the goatskin strip from around my waist. The length of it was still bandaged around the decaying thing that my limb had become. I helped her to undo some of the paraphernalia from my limb. I let her discard most of it, but not my leather strip.

The doctor examined my limb while she scribbled things on a page in her folder. I wish I could remember the small talk that the good doctor shared with me while he inspected my defeated limb. It was grey, numb and smelt worse than fresh defecation, more like the decaying body of a stray dog.

The nurse filled a silver basin with lukewarm water. She poured things in it and wheeled it over to me. She clamped small gauze swabs with the forceps and wiped and wiped from my limb. It was very uncomfortable, this whole thing. She removed chunks and chunks of what she called "debris" from my limb. Apparently, my limb was more debris than it was, in fact, a limb. She wiped and wiped some more, until she had to open a new packet of swabs. Exactly fifty-four hours later, when she had finished wiping, she smeared brown stuff with a flat wooden stick onto small squares of gauze from the pile on the tray. When the brown marmite stuff filled most of the swabs, she wrapped what was left of my limb with them. Then she bandaged me all the way round.

While she was busy, the doctor told me he would advise my grandfather to go home, because it was obvious that I was going to be admitted. He asked if I needed anything from Grandfather. I said no.

'And the blanket?' he asked.

'I'll keep it,' I replied without hesitation. What was Grandfather going to do with a stained white blanket, spotted with drops of blood, at the village?

After the nurse's treatment, I felt much more comfortable, physically. It was as if my body had been relieved of something burdensome, something heavier than just the debris. I was given a blue gown to wear that left most of my back uncovered. But I was used to nakedness. I was then wheeled off by Mr Ugly, the porter. As soon as he came in, my eyes dropped down automatically. I would not lift them up again until he'd parked me safely at ward number six.

As I entered, there was some twisting and turning from the other patients, who were asleep by then. The time must have been something to ten, although it felt like a year had passed since I'd first entered the hospital building. I was shown the panic button thing under my pillow and told to press it if I needed anything. I slid between the cold white sheets. It felt very uncomfortable to me, sleeping in a bed. I wasn't used to it. In fact, I wasn't used to sleeping at all. I must have drifted off at some stage, though, with my hand on that panic button thing. It was probably the solution in the saline bag, which they'd said would help the pain and inflammation, that knocked me out.

When I next came to consciousness, it was to the depressing knowledge that sleep had not wiped out the nightmare of my reality. Things had gone horribly wrong on the mountain, and I had failed to complete my passage into manhood. I had not become a man the supposed way.

But before I ended up what I am today, dear reader, I had a life.

2

When the schools re-opened at the beginning of the year in 2001, I enrolled at Zweledinga High School, in a village called Yonda in the Eastern Cape. I was 18 years old and commencing my grade 12; a year older than most of my classmates. That is because I had flunked grade 11 in 1999 when I was living in Cape Town.

My friend Moeketsi and I had spent more time outside the classroom than in it, playing soccer or smoking Swati *zols* in the school toilet block. The two of us rarely made it to class, except on rainy days. There was no point in staying outside the classroom when it was raining, since the only dry place you could be stationed was the toilet block. Aside from smelling bad, this increased the chance of your being bust. There was also no point in bunking class when you had no *zol*. So only on the rare occasions when it was raining and we also had no *zol* did Moeketsi and I attend class. That is why we did not get promoted to the next level.

I repeated my grade 11 in 2000 and succeeded the second time round. Coincidentally, Moeketsi's parents had withdrawn him from the school that year. I was lonely, I had no other friends there. The other bastards in my class thought they were better and cleverer than me just because I'd flunked a year. My new classmates were, in any case, too young for me; our minds were not at the same level at all.

At the end of that year my mother came to fetch me from

Cape Town. I had not seen her in years, but it had somehow reached her ears that I'd been bust twice for doing crime, and that I was smoking lots of *zol* and stuff. True, I was bust twice, once by the police, but it was nothing major.

The first incident happened with Killer and Voice, my *chommies* in Gugulethu. We were out on one of our "redistribution" missions in the rich suburbs. It was Voice who had first come up with the idea of car radios. He'd persuaded us that we could make a lot of money if we sold them. This was going to be an easier alternative to the housebreaking we were already doing – which was too risky and strenuous. With housebreaking, there was always the possibility you would have to kill or be killed. We'd been lucky so far. But we were getting increasingly anxious about our luck running out. So Killer and I bought into the new idea without hesitation. It wasn't just anyone but Voice, the mastermind, who had brought up this idea, after all. Voice was our brains. Killer was our muscle, and I contributed with my bravery. My name is Lumkile, but the other two called me Bravo.

We three were the role models of our *kasi*. When they saw us together, young boys got inspired. *Oongwana* were flattered by our attention, while the grown-ups were quiet and polite around us. This is because they knew what we were capable of, though we were always careful not to do ugly things in *ekasi*. But really, what gained us respect was that we played football.

Let me tell you, there was no Shining Stars Football Club without the three of us. That is why *Ta'*Diski, the coach, called us into his *kamer* and treated us to a long belting session when he heard of our wayward actions outside *kasi*. He was the first to suggest that what we needed was *ukwaluswa*. Among the traditional-leaning people, you know those who consult their ancestors for every little thing, *ukwaluswa* is the go-to remedy for mischievous behaviour like ours. *Ta'*Diski wasn't interested in excuses that we were starving. He just regretted the wasted talent and thought circumcision would solve everything.

The day that it all went wrong started as normal. As soon as we came back from school, my friends and I went around our little *kasi* gathering enough money for ten Swati *zols* and a twenty pack of cigarettes.

Voice, the strategist, had checked the weather and told us there was a 60 per cent chance of rain that night – perfect weather for the job. It was always safer to break into cars when it was raining, because when the weather was like that people tended to stay indoors. We usually targeted the southern suburbs in our Operation Redistribution, since lots of whites stayed there and it was well known that they were the loaded guys. Besides which, we figured they owed us something, on account of apartheid and all.

At around seven that evening, we gathered at Voice's place. The bastard had stolen 50 rand from his stepfather's wallet and bought crack with it. We collected our lumber jackets and settled down for a good thick session of smoking. I opened the session by taking first cream and Killer took seconds. Voice took his time, as usual, to stir the pipe and prepare for his own first cream. The bastard said he enjoyed watching Killer and I struggle with the first high so that he could laugh at us as we gasped for air. Killer hated first creams. They made him throw up. So, he always took seconds, and the first creams alternated between Voice and me.

We kissed the *bottle kop* several times and allowed our bodies to float to Disneyland, Hollywood and wherever else is heaven-ish. After some two hours of moistness, we dragged ourselves towards Nyanga train station. It did not take long before the last train from Khayelitsha to Cape Town arrived. We boarded free of charge, as usual.

It was understood between my friends and I that the Bravo of our group was the only animal allowed to carry a knife. We hated weapons; believe me we did. But as expected, I had my *goni* with me. It was my responsibility to protect us from any potential danger, such as stray gangsters from the Cape

Flats. But it had been a peaceful journey so far, and I hadn't needed to draw my *goni*. Our heads were still floating about in wonderland as we got off at Salt River station, heading towards Observatory. Voice warned that since there were also many darkies and coloureds living at Obz, we should rather stick to our usual hunting grounds like Rondebosch, Newlands and Plumstead, where the richer pickings were. Voice's word was final. The bastard always did his homework. So Killer and I did not question him, we just marched along.

We followed the train rails, puffing *zol* after *zol* to sustain our moistness. A drizzling rain had started. Let me tell you, you haven't had shit if you haven't smoked a *zol* in the rain. The tiny drops spat down to harass the burning of the *zol*, and I'd have to keep pulling hard to make sure it didn't go out. I was floating so much the stones under my feet felt like cushions.

When we got to Rondebosch, Voice lagged behind and then stopped, gazing at something in the distance. Killer and I knew something was up. My friends and I never needed to do much talking. We just read each other's head people. Voice was the expert at spotting targets. Killer and I took a few steps back and shot our eyes in the direction where Voice was looking. There it was; our field for the night. It was a huge City Hall, its windows all lit up. There must have been a concert or something going on there. We could hear horns and trumpets being blown with gusto from inside.

I'll bet each one of us was thinking the same thing at that moment: this is the life we want to live, too, the life of privilege and plenty. We want to attend live music concerts on Wednesdays, too. We want to afford the entry fee for a change, and we want to drive to the concerts in our own cars. We want to bring our families along, and have reserved seats. What makes white people think they deserve to be rich and us poor? What makes them think they are entitled to wealth and us to poverty? If Voice and Killer weren't thinking those things, then I at least was. I was asking myself those questions.

And the anger of knowing that no one would ever be prepared to answer them gave me the courage to go on doing what I was doing and act like the Bravo my friends expected me to be.

We walked towards the parking lot. Voice reached into his underpants and retrieved enough bombs for each of us. All three of us mouthed our bombs as I led the way through the boom gate. These bombs from the white stone pieces cracked from a car's spark plug are very useful: you could blast the driver's window without even being heard by the passenger. That little thing turns a window into a trillion pieces of glass mince in point two seconds.

Our strategy was to attack one car at a time. It made the job less messy and we could be each other's guards that way, too. We were always careful not to touch the cars that had a red flash on the dashboard. *Umgqala-gqala*, the alarm, is the mother of all fuck-ups in this game.

Voice and Killer were still creeping about, trying to survey the vulnerability of the old BMW we'd chosen, when I bombed the window. I didn't wait for any signal from the others, I simply pushed the rest of the window, which had turned into a carcass after I bombed it, onto the driver's seat and pinned the door back. That is the trick, see; you push the mince inside to minimise any noise. By the time I opened the other doors for Killer and Voice, my spare hand was already halfway into the cassette mouth of the car radio, pulling it free. 52 seconds later we were out of the *BM*, with Voice emptying out the paper contents of the UCT sports bag for us to carry our cargo in. We left the *BM* looking like *umdlongolo*, a stolen and vandalised car. We were busy on our fifth hit when the concert came to an end. Hundreds of pale faces emerged onto the open veranda, shielding themselves under huge umbrellas.

'*Sout!*' Voice whispered an alert.

We cockroached out of the vicinity without being noticed. We were still counting our blessings mentally, walking calmly on to what we thought was a safe distance away, when a police van appeared from nowhere and coasted to a halt in front of us. Its lights were off and I suspected the engine as well, since we hadn't heard a thing. A police officer screamed, 'Freeze!'

Shit! I thought.

I froze. Killer and Voice melted under the cars nearby while my hands gathered frost up in the sky. I swallowed the rest of the bombs that were in my mouth. Voice had long since dropped the cargo in the grass. That's the first thing you do, see. You can't be bust red-handed. You dump the shit and disown it like a bastard child.

It did not take long before my accomplices were hauled out of their hiding places and the three of us were bundled into the back of the police van, heading to a destination we couldn't fathom. I was already gathering courage to stand up for my stuff at Pollsmoor. I wasn't going to be one of those wife prisoners, unless the buggers gang-raped me. I dumped my *goni* in the van and a few hundred hours later, the flight landed at Goodwood police station.

The usual stuff was done, you know: fingerprints, and left-right-centre photographs. Then we were frogmarched to an empty cell. It was dark and damp. That was my first experience of prison, and I didn't like it.

The following day we were transported to Cape Town Magistrate's Court, where our names were the first to be called: Lizwi Liyazongoma, Mbulali Khabingesi and Fumanekile Mfanekisongqondweni; that was Voice, Killer and I, respectively. We'd given ourselves those pseudonyms in the van. We were asked to swear something about the truth and nothing but the truth. The man in the black gown sitting on the platform then ordered that we be given our letters of remand. The letters ordered us to appear at the court again a month later. Fortunately, we never had to; something went wrong with the evidence, and our case never came to trial.

Meanwhile, we used our letters to get access at the train stations. We produced them to the security personnel like they were Olympic medals.

So that was our first bust.

The second happened as a result of serious desperation. We'd run out of drug money and were planning to head for our usual operations area to remedy that, but unfortunately, we never got there. The last trains from Kapteinsklip and Khayelitsha to Cape Town had both been cancelled. This meant we were stranded in Gugulethu, with no transport to get us where we wanted to go. The anger that gripped us! Voice marched off furiously down the train rails. A short while later he shuffled himself back to us, defeated.

Without discussion, we turned and headed back *ekasi*. I was surprised when I saw Voice lagging behind, the sign that he had seen something. Killer and I stopped in confusion. We weren't expecting Voice to spot a potential target right in our own *kasi*. It had been our silent policy not to *bhathula* from our brothers and sisters; that thing was meant for whites. But, true, this was a very disappointed Voice we were dealing with. Killer and I took the necessary steps back to join him and tried to figure out what it was that had captured Voice's eye. I don't know about Killer, but I didn't see any potential targets among the shacks around us.

'Lizwi?' I called out Voice's name, meaning, *What the hell are you thinking?*

'There's a radio there, isn't there?' he said.

'Where?' Killer asked, although he knew where Voice was referring to. As expected, he did not get his reply. The two of us joined Voice as he marched towards Nosandla's Citi Golf. The car wasn't even locked, and it did not have *umgqala-gqala*. Voice did the job one-man. It was risky because we knew very well we would be the first suspects. But we were desperate enough to take the risk.

Later, I was at home asleep when I felt someone shaking me violently.

'Where is Nosandla's radio?' a voice roared from above me.

'*Ja... mnxm,*' I mumbled from my drugged sleep.

'Is it with you, Satan?' the voice persisted. A fist-blow descended on my head. I came awake to find my father standing over me, fuming. He was determined to get the truth from me about Nosandla's radio that, naturally, I swore I knew nothing about. He did not give me any options but ordered me to get dressed and walk with him to Nosandla's. I went into a panic when I found Voice and Killer already waiting there with their parents.

Shit! I thought.

The *flippen* cargo was right in front of Voice. I denied having anything to do with it. I wasn't about to own up to stolen goods in front of my father. As it was, that bastard was going to break my limbs when we got home. Voice and Killer covered for me like the good friends they were. They told our parents that I wasn't there when it happened. They knew the story of my father and me. After all, it was they who stole extra carcasses of food from their homes to provide for me every night, because my own father left me to starve.

The less said about my father the better.

So those were the two incidents which – I do not know how – my mother must have heard about, and which brought her all the way to Cape Town to fetch me. I got the shock of my life when she turned up so unexpected, like. I hadn't seen her in five years. In fact, I hadn't heard a word from her since she'd sent me away to go and live with my father in Gugulethu. I think she did this to save me from my uncle's abuse, for my uncle had a habit of rearranging the different parts of me.

I agreed to go with her and left the Cape for that other Cape. By that time, I'd had enough of the crazy life. I'd had enough of living in my father's shack with nothing, of being left to fend for myself for weeks at a time while he went off to stay with his girlfriend, Pinki, in her brick house on the other side of Gugulethu. I'd had enough of being beaten up by him in his drunken rages. And I'd had enough of drugs and crime, although those weren't the labels I gave them, then. I didn't want to be that person any more. I wanted a fresh start, and my mother was offering that to me.

When I got to Ngojini, my mother's village, I went clean. I stopped smoking *zol* and doing the other shit. I gave up smoking. And drinking, too. This was not my choice, you understand. In the villages, youths are treated very differently from in the city. They don't have the same freedom to do what they want, and their behaviour is much more controlled. In any case, drugs are not so easy to get hold of there.

The quiet life of the village was a real culture shock, and I can't say I didn't struggle. I had a lot of adjusting to do. But I also had a lot to prove.

I was glad when the schools reopened. This was my chance to prove to my mother – and myself – that I wasn't the terrible creature I was reported to be. I wanted to do something with my life, to work out a grand plan for my future and put it into action.

Zweledinga High School was not the best school in the world in which to achieve my goals. It might well have been one of the worst; academically, it had a very poor record and the matric failure rate was high. Physically, too, it wasn't inspiring.

It was a brown prefabricated structure located next to the sowing fields on the outskirts of the village. There was no fencing, the doors had long since been relieved of their handles, and I don't remember a single glass pane in the windows. There weren't even proper toilets; like every other structure in that school, the toilets had been stripped of their seats and all the other parts that make it a toilet. All that was left were the walls and holes. The whole school was being carted away little by little by village looters. We considered ourselves lucky to still find some structure called school every morning.

But I was determined not to let those things discourage me. I thought Zweledinga High was a good place for me to teach everybody a fucking lesson about resilience. I told myself I was going to get a university pass from that very dishonourable school they had sent me to. Come hell or high water, I was going to make it happen.

But this change of mind only came after my turning point. When I first arrived at Ngojini, all I could think about was getting out of there again as fast as I could.

3

I knew I was not far from hell as soon as the minibus taxi slowed down, preparing to exit the tarred stretch of road for the gravel strip beyond it. The plump old lady next to me tried to open the window. She knew the dust from that brown patch we called a road was going to occupy the space around us in no time, and hoped by opening a window to give it exit room. But the window was permanently immobilised.

The choking dust invaded us, powdering our skins to a smooth texture. I felt it on my teeth and tongue, even though I hadn't opened my mouth all this while. It even came through my nostrils.

We rattled our way along the corrugated road down to the village. I saw the two pointy mountains beneath which our village lay. They are shaped in such a way that you could imagine them to be the breasts of a sixteen-year-old girl. Our village is located right at the cleavage of these breasts.

Below the village is the Ox-Kraal dam. It's like the bladder of this girl on whose cleavage our village is placed. After rainfall the water descends from the breasts down the furrow that cleaves our village, to fill the Ox-Kraal bladder. At night the water looks like a trillion litres of breast milk in the starlight.

We used to drink from this dam in the olden days, until we were weaned from it by Mandela.

We now have taps on each dusty street. Our water comes from a borehole, and there is electricity as well.

I noted all these things as we finally descended from the chicken-shed-in-transit that we called a minibus taxi. Mother and I were transformed into browner creatures than when we'd started, thanks to the dust.

The first thing that caught my eye was the graveyard. I saw numerous fresh graves on the far side, and wondered the obvious.

Somehow, when you looked at the graveyard, you could not prevent your head people from predicting where you might be laid in the future. I did my calculations by generation. The generation of Grandfather would lay up there, then that of Mother somewhere towards that tree, and our own generation would probably be down there, next to the fence. These predictions were never very accurate, though, since people tended to die randomly rather than sequentially.

The giant pine tree from which my uncle had once attempted to hang himself was still there as custodian of the graves. No one knew why he had done it. Such things are not talked about in village culture, at least not openly. The grey tombstone, the biggest of them all, was also still there, right at the heart of the graveyard. We were led to believe it was Jesus's tombstone. The Moravian church is big here, and according to them, this is where Jesus emerges from, every Resurrection Day.

Over there was the Moravian church building. Another giant pine tree was planted in front of its whitewashed facade. There were two black crows flying back and forth between the two trees. I found something almost evil about the way they flew to and fro like that, between graveyard and church, transporting whatever it was from church to the graves; or worse, the other way round. The head people imagined them to be journalists, carrying bad news.

A few metres away from the church building stood the arch of the big church bell. It was whitewashed, too, as were the stones framing the road to the church. The church bell also served as a knell for the village. When someone died, *Oom*

Dan, who was Grandfather's brother-in-law, was entrusted with the responsibility of ringing the knell. He did it so perfectly you could never mistake it for any other bell-ringing: *ting... ting... ting* (pause) *ting... ting... ting* (pause) *ting... ting... ting*. That was the anthem for those who wouldn't make it to lunch that day.

The whole village became arrested by palpitations when Dan rang that bell. Our head people did a collective search for the victim. Could it be *gogo* so-and-so, or was it the sick father of so-and-so? No, it must be the disabled daughter of so-and-so, or the new-born of so-and-so's child.

As youngsters, sitting around the brazier, we used to bet on it. I always bet on the *gogos*. They were the ones rumoured to be witches and I was afraid of them. *Oom* Dan was the only one who could settle our bets. He took his time to knock on each door in the village to let the grown-ups know who it was that he had rung the knell for.

It didn't matter if the message reached him at two in the morning that someone had just passed on, *Oom* Dan got up and did his thing anyway. Now if you couldn't wait until daylight to hear, as was often the case, then you had to put your lamps on to indicate to *Oom* Dan that you were, in fact, awake. He would descend from the church to your house to announce the sad loss of so-and-so. Actually, most of the villagers put their lamps on. Curious people, my villagers! But I realise that it was also a safety measure, you know. Otherwise you could murder the whole village inside your skull between the time the knell had rung and sunrise when you got to hear.

We children had to eavesdrop near the grown-ups' room while *Oom* Dan relayed the story of the latest sad loss. Yes, it was always that: a sad loss. We, the children, didn't see it that way. To us it was just death. There was nothing sentimental about it. But grown-ups are very dramatic people.

They have this tendency to talk in riddles, too. Everything had to be said in a roundabout way, never directly. The

result was that if *Oom* Dan began his door-to-door rounds at
sunrise, he would finish the 300 homes of our village in the
late afternoon. I suppose he also had tea and things in each
and every house.

'Death in this place is so imminent these days, *bhut'* Dan,'
Grandmother would greet him, getting straight to the point
of where her interest lay. Grandmother had no patience with
waiting through the usual roundabout way of things. She is
like that, my grandmother: direct.

'That is the truth, *Sbalikazi*, that is the truth,' Dan would
agree, but still not pronounce the sad loss's identity; not that
easily. *Oom* Dan referred to my grandmother as *Sbalikazi* –
sister-in-law – since he had married my grandfather's older
sister, Kholiswa.

'Yes, *Sbali*,' Grandfather would join in at this stage. 'You
know... mmh... in the old days... mmh... people used to die
of old age. Today... mmh... today, this youth dies like flies,'
he would say.

'If you know flies, *Sbali*,' *Oom* Dan would agree, adding
some more flies.

'Like flies, *tata*.' Grandmother would add a few flies of her
own, in resignation. At this point she would leave the room to
make some tea.

'Flies, *Sbalikazi*.' *Oom* Dan would add some extra leftover
flies, as if to allow her time to leave the room.

'Mmh...' Grandfather would sigh then pause, while a
hacking cough shook him. 'Flies, *Sbali*,' he would say again, as
if in agreement with *Oom* Dan's delaying tactics, followed by
more coughing.

As a small boy, eavesdropping, you would be lost in these fly
riddles. Like grandmother, you just wanted to know who had
passed away, so that you could sort out your bets.

'How are they doing at home, *Sbali*?' Grandfather would
enquire of his brother-in-law. *Oom* Dan would then take the
time to narrate the mischief of his eldest son who stole his

neighbour's goat. He'd tell about the stroke that was taking its toll on his wife. And the recent bird disease outbreak that saw his chicken shed left vacant.

'It is as I say, *Sbali*,' he would conclude.

'Mmh... I see, *Sbali*.' There would be silence.

'As for the matter of the boy, *Sbali*, the solution is obvious,' Grandfather would declare.

'The obvious you say, *Sbali*?'

'Mmh... the obvious, *Sbali*,' Grandfather would insist.

According to the elders, if a boy reached a stage where he was problematic in society, there was only one way to curb this, and that was "the obvious". The boy's mischief was an indication of wanting a rite of passage into manhood. The things that were done at the mountain were held to be so powerful that they could root out any foolish notions from a boy's stubborn head, sending him back with a clear sense of right and wrong.

'I am considering it, *Sbali*. I am,' Dan would say.

'Mmh... you will have done yourself and my sister a good turn if you solve it as a matter of urgency, *Sbali*. My nephew is not getting any younger, after all. You don't want the surgeon to have to use a saw, now do you? Mmh...'

'You are advising me, *Sbali*. You are.'

'Send the boy this next December, *Sbali*.'

'This next December?'

'Next December, *Sbali*.'

'*Sbali*, we accord too much time to the matter of this boy. The dog would smile to learn that his fathers here abandon important matters that eat the world, only to talk about its little skin.'

'*Gagaga... gagaga... gagaga*,' they would laugh.

'*Gukru... gukru... gukru*.' The laughter would turn into compulsive coughs.

'Yes (*gukru*), *Sbali*. How is my *Sbali* doing this side?' *Oom* Dan would ask Grandfather.

'Mmh... *Sbali*, ailments, *Sbali*, ailments.'

'Yes, *Sbali*. Ailments. How can I forget ailments, *Sbali*?'

'*Gagaga... gagaga... gaaaagaga...* ailments, *Sbali... gaaagaga... gagaga.*' Again they would do harm to laughter, until laughter did harm to them.

It wouldn't be until Grandmother came back in with the tea that *Oom* Dan would turn to the real purpose of his visit. As a child, you would be bored to death by that time with these riddles of flies, surgeons, ailments and the like.

On the day I arrived from Cape Town, it felt like my life had come to a complete halt as I thought back to these things. Everything was just the same as it had always been – still, silent and old-fashioned. It bored the stuff out of me. I had forgotten the way it was here. I could not fathom a life in a place like this. I told myself that was it: I was going to behave well just to buy time and a little bit of trust before I made my way back *ekasi*. I wasn't prepared to start milking cows, shepherding sheep and all those other rural things. I'd done a lot of that when I was growing up in this place, and I wasn't about to go back to that backward life now. I was used to the groove and style of *kasi*; I needed speed, noise, action. It was the new millennium after all, and life was for the living, not the wasting. First chance I got, I would be heading back to Cape Town, where I belonged.

4

My mother and I never really had a relationship. She was a schoolteacher based at a school in the Transkei, so she didn't come home, except during the holidays. Growing up, I felt that she wasn't there to parent me. And during the years that I spent at my father's place in Cape Town, we had no communication. So we didn't really know each other at all.

When she came to fetch me from Cape Town, we never discussed the trouble that had brought her there. She asked me no questions about it. The day she arrived, I'd overheard an exchange between her and my father. He'd been ranting about me and my "criminal" behaviour. But all she said was: 'Children, children, they're all the same.' Her calm reaction had impressed me deeply. I'd felt that she understood me, and didn't judge me. It was part of the reason why I'd agreed to go back with her. Now, I was sorry that things hadn't worked out for me in Ngojini, for I would have liked to have got to know her better.

About two weeks after my return to the village, I began to prepare my exit strategy. I started to mumble things about going back to Cape Town. I didn't tell anyone in particular, I just threw things into the air. I trusted the wind to transport what I was mumbling to Mother's ears. I was expecting her to be furious on hearing of my intentions, or at least show some negative reaction. But not my mother.

'I hear you are making plans to go back to Cape Town, my boy,' she said to me one morning.

'Right, moms,' I replied, in the cocky lingo of the township.

'When exactly?'

'In two weeks' time. Just before school re-opens.'

I smiled as I said this. It seemed I was succeeding in getting my way much more easily than I had anticipated.

My mother gave me a searching look. 'I hope you know what you're doing, Lumkile,' she said. 'But if that's what you want I have no objection. I would like to give you a gift, something to take back with you, since I don't know when I'll see you again. Tell me, my boy, what would you like? What is it that you need most in your life?'

I had never been asked such a thing before. Me? What did I need? In the five years I spent with my father I never felt I had any choices. Things were obligatory. It was not a matter of me doing what I wanted, I just had to do the things I was ordered to do. It was never about me, it was about him, his girlfriend Pinki, them. Although I couldn't name the thing I needed most in my life, I was sure I knew what it was. It was always there in my forehead. Sometimes, not getting that thing made me weep alone at night, made me wish that I was dead. Now here I was being asked to spell it out by my mother.

'Uh-mm...' I attempted to put it into words. But it did not come out. What was it again, that thing I wanted and needed the most? That thing that sent me breaking into white people's houses. Stealing radios from cars. That made me keep my head in a constant state of moisture. Wasn't it the *kasi* life... style, noise, action?... No, *maan*, it was bigger, that thing.

My mother continued to look at me. Without saying anything she went to her bag and retrieved her purse from it, the small black one. She emptied it on top of her bed. I had never seen so many orange 200-rand notes before. A broad grin grew on my face. So much money! She asked me to help count it and put it into money bags.

She put a tag on each bag. On the fat one in which she had

asked me to put 3000 rand, she stuck a tag on which was scribbled my full name: Lumkile Chris Vumindaba, together with the amount and the purpose of the money. The 3000 rand was budgeted for my pocket money. My palms had gathered sweat. I couldn't believe the gift she had given me. What I felt was not gratitude so much as amazement. Money, to me, was something to steal or to have stolen from me. But here was I with three Gs of my own in my pocket.

I learned to say thank you that night. Seriously, I was not used to it. In my life so far, there had never been much to thank anyone for. But that night, as the chest people sat in my throat, I said thank you to my mother as if it was the first time I had ever said the words.

I spent the next day sitting with jelly knees on my bed, trying to recover from this new shock in my life. I counted and recounted the cash. I put it in the wardrobe, under the mattress, in my pants, everywhere. There were even times when I lost it and had to search for it while drenched in a cold sweat. Only to find it exactly where I'd hidden it the last time: in the ceiling.

The following day I went shopping in Queenstown. I bought myself two pairs of Levis jeans at Sales House, one navy and one brown. I got myself a pair of red All Star *takkies* from the same shop, and a Starter T-shirt and Pierre Cardin cap that were on sale. With those things, I was going to be a sure hit *ekasi* when I returned there. I walked around a bit and I found myself at KFC. This was the very first time that I was about to buy myself something to eat that I chose. I *sommer* got a Streetwise Two. When I was done, I perambulated about for a while, looking for something, though I wasn't sure what, exactly. I suddenly did not have the desire for anything else in town. Honestly. I had everything I needed, and still more than half the cash unspent.

On my way back to the taxi rank, I saw a liquor store and went in. The white man behind the counter must have asked me what I wanted at least a dozen times. I did not have an answer for him. I knew I did not need to dilute this joyful feeling inside me. So I left the liquor store, dry. Can you believe it?

In the taxi, there was a man sitting near me who smelt of a combination of beer and smoke. He just wouldn't be quiet, and every time he opened his mouth, I could not take the smell. It was like I'd suddenly developed an allergy to booze and fags. I swapped seats.

Then there was this other guy who had an attitude thing going on, calling the grandmothers in the taxi *"o'lady"* this and *"o'lady"* that. He made me *naar*. Couldn't he refer to elders properly? He made the mistake of glancing my way from under his cap. I gave him that look. The *kasi* look. The kind that strips you of arrogance, quietens you down and activates anxiety in you. It lets you know that you're in harm's way. That's the look I gave this guy. He dropped his eyes immediately. I held the stare unblinking until the *bharu* looked up at me again. He saw the snake eyes were still on him and gave up, shutting his big mouth and covering his pimpled face with his cap. But I remained angry. If there's one thing I can't stand, it's a grown man being disrespectful to women old enough to be his grandmothers.

I battled with myself, trying to readjust my mood and recover the elation I'd been feeling earlier. But the pimpled guy with his disrespect had spoilt the day.

I was further disturbed by the sight of initiates from Sada township sitting there in open view at the bus shelter beside the main road with their blankets and white clay faces and knobkerries, asking for money from women. This was an abominable act to me. What was wrong with everyone? Why were people so determined to go against the proper way of doing things? *No wonder it is all falling apart*, I found myself thinking.

When I got home, I surprised myself by stripping down

in front of my mother and young siblings to try on my new things. It was like I was a child again.

After that, I went to clean my room. Here in Ngojini I had my own room, unlike in Cape Town, where I had to share a shack with my father. When *sis'*Pinki visited, which was often, I heard things I wasn't meant to. Those things wounded me inside. I didn't have to put up with any of that here in my grandfather's house. The house was big enough for all of us: grandfather, grandmother, mother, uncle, my two young siblings and me. All the adults had their own bedrooms, and I was allocated my own as well. It was slowly dawning on me that I had a lot to be grateful for, here.

That day marked the beginning of my new life. My mother's gift had changed everything. It was not so much the 3000 rand she had given me, but what it signified. I understood that the money was an expression of the regret and love she felt for me.

That night we spoke properly for the first time. 'On hearing some of the stories of what was going on with you in Cape Town, I felt pain in my abdomen,' she told me. 'It was the same physical pain that pierced me seventeen years ago when I gave birth to you. The head people wouldn't let me rest after I received the news about you. I was guilt-stricken. I wept myself to sleep that night. I asked God to give me a second chance to mother you, and came to reclaim you from the custody of your father. I was greatly relieved to find you without a single scar on your face and was most pleased to see a different picture of you from what I'd been told you were. I thank God for protecting you on my behalf. You are my firstborn son and you cannot be replaced. I want you to know that I love you with all my being.'

Her words brought me to tears. My mother was being a mother to me. It dawned on the head people that this, here, was the thing I had wanted, the thing I had craved more than any other thing. I didn't need to go anywhere. I had what I needed, right here.

5

The following day I went shopping again. This time I bought the fitted grey pants, two white shirts, black Crocket & Jones shoes and navy tie of Zweledinga High School. Since it had dawned on the head people that right here in Ngojini was the life I could claim as my own, my whole approach to things had changed. Whereas before I'd seen school and schoolwork as a torture to be avoided at all cost, I now regarded it as an opportunity for a better life. I didn't want to just sleepwalk through my life the way I had before. I wanted to make something of myself. I set targets and worked hard to achieve them. And for the first time, I experienced the pleasure of success.

It wasn't only my schoolwork that reflected this change in attitude. I began to take better care of myself too, to pay more attention to my appearance and personal hygiene. I kept a nail cutter in my bag and used some of my leftover money to purchase a Wahl machine so that I could renew my bald every fifth day. My school uniform was always clean and ironed and I shined my CJ shoes obsessively. These days, I liked the guy in the mirror – and the one reflected in people's corneas when they looked at me.

I worked hard in class, always hounded by the sense that I was behind with time. Although I was satisfied with my results, I was not complacent. I studied constantly, chasing excellence, trying to make up for the time I'd lost.

I began to think beyond where my feet were standing. In *kasi*, the head people were constantly caught up in a jumble of thoughts on how to resolve the immediate crisis. It was always about overcoming the next obstacle. Life was instantaneous, abrupt, fast and always in climax. The scene of *kasi* is the crux of the young black story in South Africa.

The speed, noise, action thing was about that: the here and now. It was a revolving-door-syndrome kind of life. You circled and circled to no end. Well, that's not strictly true – there was an end. Actually, two ends: Pollsmoor or NY5. You either ended up doing time in prison, or they buried you, or both. That is the inevitable destination for many young black people in *kasi*. There is no peaceful conclusion or happy ending to that kind of life. I was lucky to have got out when I did, though just how lucky, I didn't realise until later.

One day I phoned my cousin in *kasi* to catch up on news. When I asked about Voice and Killer, I could not believe what I heard in answer. My cousin told me in her matter-of-fact way that it was now two months since Voice had been taken away by the police. It turned out he had murdered one of the small-timers called Nkanki. Yes, Voice had killed another human being! I resisted prompting for more details. I suppose the head people were closing that *kasi* door. But it wasn't without difficulty. All my cousin told me was that Nkanki had been caught red-handed stealing some of Voice's *goetes*. Voice had been so angry that he'd stabbed him 36 times.

Later, I found out the rest of the story from other *kasi* cronies. They said that when Voice's father came out of his shack after the police had taken his son away, he'd been shocked to witness so many people surrounding his house. The crowd had begun to spew insults and curses at him for his good job of raising such a skilled murderer.

Stones were thrown at him, along with bottles and pieces of plank. Then his shack was set alight, and Voice's father was punched and booted and left next to the raging flames.

The crowd began to sing revolutionary songs and *toyi-toyi* in protest, demonstrating their no-nonsense attitude to the crime. They then moved towards Killer's house. He wasn't there, but a word of warning – no, thousands of words of warning were said to his parents.

Inevitably, the *toyi-toyi* mob had marched on to my father's house. They found no response to their shouts. The door was shut and the shack was empty. Someone in the crowd recalled that my father had been seen holding hands with *sis'*Pinki further down the street a short while before. A million words of warning were left with my father's neighbours. My father must have been shocked to discover a half brick inside his bedroom on his return, and the window transformed into mince.

When the *toyi-toyi* dissolved, the one and only street of *kasi* was left wounded and lonesome. The firefighters had managed to kill the fire at Voice's place, but too late. The shack was ashes, and his father was dead. The smoke formed a dark cloud above *kasi* that dimmed the brightness of the February noon. That was the one time at our *kasi* that the sun set at midday, literally.

Things didn't end there. Early on the morning of Nkanki's funeral, Killer was finally found. He'd run away on the day Voice was collected by the police. Seven days later, he was found in front of his house, bundled up in a Shoprite trolley, his head and torso shrouded with a white flour sack. His father had gone to see who it was under the sack. He thought at first that they'd murdered Killer and delivered his body in the trolley. But Killer wasn't dead. He was naked and mutilated. His penis had been circumcised horribly. It looked like it had been roasted and then the skin peeled off the shaft.

Killer's face was smeared with calamine lotion and his eyes were fixed in a white, unblinking stare. He has never uttered a single word since that time. I heard they sent him to Groote Schuur for treatment, then committed him to Valkenberg psychiatric hospital.

Hearing what had happened to my friends drove home to me what a lucky escape I'd had. What with Voice in prison and Killer losing his marbles, I probably would have been the one to make it to NY5 as a corpse. It was that realisation that saw me channelling all my energy into my studies. I felt I owed it to myself to choose a better ending for my life.

It was at that point that I began to take a serious look at my future, albeit with blurry eyes. There was no five-year plan on my table. The future, even thinking about such a thing, was still a new idea to me. I sat down and pondered over my current situation. My studies were going well, and if things went according to plan, I was due for circumcision at the end of that year. Then, with luck, I would be off to university and from there – who knew? I was satisfied with this draft grand plan so far. It had direction and purpose, and it gave me the impetus to study even harder than before.

It was round about this time that I allowed certain other thoughts to invade the spare faculties of the head people. I began to think about birds. And I don't mean the flying kind.

6

It was during that year that I fell in love for the first time. Her name was Yanda and she lived in Mbekweni, the village between Ngojini and Yonda, where our school was.

We were both commuters on the same bus. I boarded at 7am at the graveyard bus stop opposite the Moravian church building, and at ten past, the bus reached Mbekweni, arriving at Yonda at 7.40am. There were other students from Zweledinga High School who shared the bus ride with us. Some of them were our classmates, but I was friends with none of them. I joined in their small talk and laughed at their village jokes, but it was clear to me that we weren't going to strike up any lasting friendship. I despised their clumsy ways and stupid conversation; even more, their lack of good hygiene and grooming. This was something that had become inexcusable to me since my own conversion.

Our school had a beautiful uniform: white shirt with grey trousers for the boys and grey skirt for the girls; navy tie with white stripes, thick for the boys and thin for the girls; navy V-neck jersey with two white stripes along the collar and around the wrists; navy knee-high socks with two white stripes around the edges. There was also a school tracksuit that you could wear any day except Mondays. I took pride in our smart uniform, and it annoyed me that these noisemakers treated it with such contempt. They were determined to do all they could to spoil the splendour. Their unwashed bodies exuded

the strong smell of tobacco and sweat, and they always had
their shirts hanging out their pants. No tie was ever knotted
around their collars, and it never dawned on them that
shoelaces were made for a reason. Nor did they figure out the
purpose of owning a comb, toothbrush or nail cutter, let alone
deodorant. Their conversation was similarly "unwashed".

Everything was "*la way*" to them. The teachers were either
"*lo mjita*" or "*la way*". Really now, how can you refer to your
teachers as "this boy" and "that thing"? '*Eish, kanjani la way* that
teaches isiXhosa,' they moaned in reference to the isiXhosa
mistress. '*Eish lo mjita* of Maths *uyadika*,' they complained
about the Mathematics teacher.

For themselves, they reserved the term "*le kaka*". '*Eish le kaka
le... waaa ga- gaga, eish le kaka*,' they laughed among themselves.
Imagine people addressing each other as that: the human
dropping! But if you analysed the situation closely, you would
find that the sewage terminology they used for each other
wasn't misplaced.

I didn't find it hygienic or wise to offend my sense of smell
with so much defecation spewed carelessly. I couldn't imagine
myself as "*le kaka*" either. Not these days, anyway. So I left the
sewers to their rotten conversation in the back row of the bus
while I sat somewhere in the middle, near the emergency exit
window.

I always chose the left-hand side, so that I could watch Yanda
as she ran to the Prices Dale bus stop, which was right beside
her house. She was always late and the driver invariably had
to stop for her way past the bus stop. Her grandmother would
be standing on the red *stoep* of their face brick house, watching
her granddaughter chasing our Mayibuye. There was pride in
the way she stood, upright, her hands clasped together against
her midriff.

Unlike the rowdy boys that occupied the back of the bus,
Yanda was always exquisite in her uniform. She did not use
a bag of any sort but carried her books in her hands, hugging

them against her breast with one hand and carrying a fat pencil case in the other. She was different from the rest of the girls in many ways. She had a ready smile, not the superficial arrogance or flirting that you got from other schoolgirls.

If you were one of the guys already on the bus, you damn well wished she would select the seat next to you. But you might as well have buried that thought in your box of unfulfilled dreams, since it would never happen. Yanda would dust off her chosen seat, hug her books to her and direct her serene eyes at the view through the window. She did not indulge in gossip. She sat quietly, watching the scenery of mountains covered with thorn bush, marvelling at the greenness of the sowing fields below the mountain and swaying this way and that as the bus bellowed and rattled on to our destination.

When the bus came to a halt, only when it had come to a complete halt, would she stand up, tug at her skirt to make sure it wasn't showing too much leg at the back, and then tip-tap her way out of the big tank we called a bus.

If you were the dropout guy heading to the grazing land and you saw her walking along the small path, you damn sure knew you were missing good stuff at school. You would notice that her skirt did not reveal enough above the knees. Her long navy socks narrowed the gap of possible flesh-showing even further. Her shirt collar was strangled with the navy tie and her plastic-covered books were held close to her chest against the navy school jersey.

You would be forgiven if your cattle strayed to the sowing fields, running amok there while you marvelled at the smoothness of her face and her raw-pear body shape. Her rosy lips seemed to have been dipped in a thirst-quenching fruit juice.

If you were the grade eight boy who rang the bell at school, you would be forgiven for exceeding your bell-ringing time as you watched her jog onto the school premises.

If you were the male teacher, you would be pardoned, sir,

for never missing a single one of your double periods this year
– a thing you were infamous for. Your sudden enthusiasm for
walking between desks would be understood.

When I looked at Yanda, at the way she was, the way she
carried herself, it was as if I glimpsed a hint of brightness at the
end of the dark tunnel that was my love life. What she thought
of me, I had no idea. Or whether she even noticed me at all.
It was well into the school year, April, I think, before we had
our first conversation.

It was a rainy autumn day. The morning had started warm and
bright but the weather changed suddenly, as it does in April.
It became sullen and stormy, like the mood of a 16-year-old.
Our classmates from Chibini and Sihlabeni, the two villages
across the wide river, were excused and sent home early, for
it was well known that they wouldn't be able to cross the river
for days if it rained too hard.

The thunder blast was deafening and there were flashes of
lightning all around us. The sky was full of heavy cloud and it
grew dark, into a premature evening. The principal decided
to release us all 30 minutes ahead of time so that we could get
home before the rain came. The classroom emptied quickly
as everyone ran to the village to seek shelter with friends.
Only Yanda and I stayed behind. Neither of us had friends in
Yonda village, and our bus wasn't due for another 40 minutes.

The rain had begun to come down on the faraway mountain,
known as Kumthwakazi – Place of Plenty Bushmen. It was a
swirling white drizzle that swallowed up everything and came
sweeping towards the village. I smelt the mud, the scent of
it carried towards us on the wind. Its freshness was calming.
Yanda and I stood in the doorway of the classroom, avoiding
eye contact. It had grown even darker outside and the air was
full of the suspense of the coming storm. People were running
everywhere, some hastening to take cover, others putting out
pails to collect the rainwater. Goats were galloping down from

the mountain, calves calling for their mothers, and the music
of the rain growing ever louder as it came.

I saw that Yanda had begun to shiver. Her face was pale with
cold and her bare arms were gathering gooseflesh. She wore
just a shirt, no jersey. I retrieved the top of my tracksuit from
my satchel and offered it to her. She looked at me then and
smiled.

'What?' I asked.

'You stay with your grandmother?'

I nodded and heard her brief chuckle. She was laughing at
me for having both my jersey and tracksuit top with me. Now
that she'd mentioned it, it did seem a little *gogo*-inspired.

'Let's find somewhere else to wait,' I said.

'Where?' she asked.

'Staffroom,' I suggested.

I packed her books and pencil case into my 18 Litre
Karrimor school bag and we sprinted together for the prefab
staffroom. The teachers were surprised to learn that the two
of us were still there.

'What were the two of you so busy doing when the others
packed their things and left?' *la way* of isiXhosa enquired
accusingly.

'They went to friends in the village, Miss,' I answered.

'That's not what I asked. Have you a hearing problem,
mfana?'

'No, Miss,' I said.

La way turned to Yanda. 'And you, why do you not answer
for yourself? Is he your spokesperson-cum-boyfriend?' she
said.

I was glad that Yanda did not reply to that. I looked at her
and she was unable to hold back her laughter at the stupidity
of *la way* of isiXhosa. I must admit, the "cum-boyfriend" bit
was funny.

After this grilling, we were given a key to the teachers'
meeting room, with strict instructions to behave ourselves in

there. The two of us collapsed into hysterical laughter as soon as I locked the door behind us. I put my bag down while Yanda pulled her socks up above her knees. We laughed some more at this spectacle. Then she pulled the sleeves of the tracksuit top down to cover her cold hands and held them in her fists. Once again, we laughed at her manoeuvres.

The storm had finally reached us. It was raining huge hailstones, and they were knocking down against the prefab roof, slowly at first, then gradually increasing in pace and volume, until their noise must have reached a thousand decibels. It sounded like a giant round of applause that went on and on. Yanda put her fists against her ears to protect her eardrums. She looked at me with an odd smile, then used her fists to push my hands up to my ears, too. I nodded to show I understood and shielded my eardrums with my thumbs. Immediately, the din of the hailstones disappeared, and it sounded as if I was hearing strange whispers instead. Yanda and I looked at each other, my thumbs in my ears and her fists over hers. And it felt like I was in this world where only she and I could hear stuff. I glanced through the staffroom window and saw that the mist of the rain had cast its white shadow over the village. And it felt like there was no one alive except the two of us.

I caught Yanda's eye again.

'Have got you a hearing problem?' I said to her jokingly.

'Whaaat?'

'Have you got a...' I motioned with my hands to indicate hearing, '... problem?'

'Whaaat?'

This silly game brought our faces close; very close. There was a silence. Then I planted my lips on hers and our mouths locked. We dissolved into each other and flew to seventh heaven.

7

I dreamed about Yanda that night. I took my dream to be my subconscious playing out the continuation of that encounter with her in the staffroom. In my dream, as in reality, we'd kissed and kissed. And the rain had sounded a huge round of applause at this spectacle.

Yanda entangled me in her arms, wrapping them around my neck. Her lips were juicy, and I'd enjoyed the uninhibited way she'd kissed me back. I held her body in my hands and we caressed each other, stumbling over chairs and other things in our way, until I guided her body down onto the boardroom table. The table was waist high. It allowed our groins to get familiar with each other. I let her lie back on the table, her legs swinging over the edge, while I stood and admired her beauty. I marvelled at the shininess of her short afro. I took pleasure in her naturalness: the un-tweezed eyebrows and un-pierced ears.

'You make me shy, staring at me like that,' she said. She hooked her finger into the collar of my school jersey and pulled me down towards her so we could resume kissing. Her breasts rubbed against my flat trunk and my hardness reached up to probe under her skirt, lurking against her warm thighs while we kissed. I touched her breasts with my hand, mesmerised by their firmness, then reached for the zip at the rear of her skirt and pulled it down in slow motion. She didn't protest, and I felt her slim fingers gripping my hardness through my

clothing. She widened her eyes at its bulkiness, and I felt a
spurt of manly pride. Her eager hands reached for my belt
and my pants descended, then my briefs. I'd already undone
her wardrobe, too. There was sensational tenderness, and a
bit of fumbling, as we each parted ways with our innocence. I
felt delicious weakness in my joints and allowed my body to
collapse on top of hers. We lay holding each other, listening
to the rock concert going on inside our chests, revelling in our
delightful soreness.

Later we dressed and lay on our backs on the boardroom
table, looking up idly at the white ceiling, as if to find the
meaning of our bodies. For my part, I'd been arrested with
shock at the discovery of the weirdness of real sex. It hadn't
been the way I'd always imagined it would be; it had been
much better.

'Look...' Yanda said, pointing to the mist that covered
the boardroom windows. They were all steamed up. She
separated herself from me and went to stand next to one of
the windows. Liberating her left hand from the sleeve of the
tracksuit top, she began to write in the mist that covered the
window:

'My first time...'

'I guessed that,' I wrote in response on the back window.

'Twas perfect but sore,' she wrote.

'Get used to it. It's normal for the first time to be sore,' I
said.

'So, you're used to it?'

'No, it's what the gents say,' I told her truthfully.

'You mean...'

'Yes, don't laugh, it's my first time, too.'

'Liar!'

'Have you got a hearing problem?' I joked, and we laughed
hysterically. Then we covered our mouths, realising that the
rain had stopped and we'd be heard by the teachers.

Then the dream took us outside, wandering hand in hand

towards the bus shelter. The rain had cleansed the atmosphere and the soil, everything seemed to be enjoying the post-climax pleasure after the storm. The muddiness of the ground swamped our school shoes and we could hear the booming sound of rainwater as it tumbled down the mountain slopes.

'Oh, cute,' Yanda said, stopping suddenly. She pointed upwards at the choreographed patterns of the flock of white birds as they flew westwards. As we stood watching them, the white station wagon that carried the teachers floated past us. *La way* was inside it, wagging her finger at us in suspicion.

Next, we were on the bus, hugging and kissing, relishing the softness of our lips rubbing against each other. Killer, my *kasi* friend, who was our driver, drove at a snail's pace through the slippery mud of the road. Our journey felt like a limousine treat.

We descended together at my graveyard stop opposite the Moravian church. The dogs came to meet us, jumping up at us in relief at our safe return. Yanda's grandmother stood watching us from the *stoep* of our house.

Somewhere, far away, a cock was crowing. Another answered. Their repeated *kikilikiki-ing* floated nearer and nearer, pulling me into wakefulness.

I checked the time and saw that it was just past four. Dawn was still two hours off, but I felt too wide awake to fall asleep again. I heard the resounding roar as rainwater descended down the swollen river towards Ox-Kraal dam. It was the same roar Yanda and I had listened to in my dream.

I got up to open the curtains to look outside.

'Wow,' the head people whispered. They were impressed at the sight of the sky with its spectacular half-moon and fine sprinkling of stars. The village was still asleep, dark and peaceful. There was an innocence about the lack of streetlights and night noise here that you didn't get in the city. The only sounds were the natural ones.

I listened to the crowing exchange between the cocks on

our side of the village and those on the other side, creating the incomprehensible conversation between birds at dawn. I thought about my dream, reliving the most pleasurable parts of it. It had felt so real, and it didn't matter to me that it wasn't. I was pleased with the way it had gone nonetheless. I knew I was in love, and it was a wonderful feeling.

8

I stood at my usual graveyard bus stop, watching the sun emerge from behind the mountain while I waited for the 7am bus to arrive. The air was fresh and clean after the rain, and around me was the usual hubbub of a rural morning, the symphony of barks, bellows, bleats and crowing indicative of a village awake.

The white station wagon that shuttled the teachers went gunning past me as it chased towards Yonda, its rear end sprayed with mud. As in my dream, I imagined I saw *la way* inside it, wagging an accusing finger at me through the window.

The bus came and I boarded. My heart beat faster as we approached Mbekweni village. Yanda emerged from her house, late as usual, cuddling her books as she ran towards the Prices Dale bus stop. I couldn't believe she was still wearing the oversized tracksuit top that belonged to me. Her grandmother popped out of their face brick house and stood on the red *stoep*, her folded hands resting against her shawled waist. The bus pulled away and Yanda stumbled a little, bumping against the seats as her eyes searched for her co-conspirator. All heads turned as she took the seat beside me. Even the noisy crew at the back was silenced.

We kissed hello. Then she pointed back through the window.

'Look at him, he is so gay,' she said.

'Who?' I asked in confusion, looking for the non-existent person she was pointing at.

'Days, the dog,' she grinned. I laughed uncontrollably at this piece of information. She was crazy, this Yanda. I mean, who notices stuff like the sexual orientation of a dog? I looked back at the black and white dog called Days as it sat with bent head, licking away at its morning hardness. I asked her how she had arrived at such a conclusion about the dog's sexuality.

'See what he's doing? He does stuff like that every morning. It's so *snaaks*, you know. He doesn't go out and chase skirt on the streets like other dogs do, he follows Grandmother from house to house as she goes about her errands. And look at the way he twists his waist as he walks; see?' Holding my neck with her warm hands, she turned my head to look out the window. It was true. The dog had that limp waist thing going on. It was funny.

'It's just a dog going dog,' I said.

'So you say.'

'C'mon, babes.'

'No. What will you say when I tell you this dog refuses to go outside when I'm taking a bath...?'

'You see, the dog is not gay. Why would it scout your girlness if it was a *moffie*? And there you have your answer about him not chasing the bitches in the street, too. He's used to seeing the contents of human skirt,' I joked.

I collected a good slap on the face for that suggestion.

'And what kind of a dog name is Days anyway?' I asked.

'Oh, that. He's named after the soap opera, you know, *Days of Our Lives*. You must see that dog when it's time for the soapies. Thieves can pack away our whole house while he stares at the TV screen. Really.'

She saw my sceptical face. 'Don't be so stubborn, admit the dog is gay. He doesn't do anything like other dogs, I told you.' This time, I collected a crispy kiss for my stubbornness.

After we'd kissed the gay-dog joke away, Yanda went silent. Then she said: 'I couldn't sleep last night.'

'Because of Days?'

'No. Because I was thinking.'

Her joking mood had changed. She began to talk about some of her worries. She was worried about us, she said, this relationship of ours; the timing of it was bad. For her, this was supposed to be a year of mending. Something like that. But we weren't able to complete our conversation because our bus had arrived at Yonda.

I took her books and stuffed them in my Karrimor bag.

'*Hayi ke mna*. I want to sit with you today,' Yanda said, as we walked into our classroom. Our teacher wasn't there that morning. And as luck would have it, MC-Squared, my tall, skinny deskmate was also absent. That's his name, MC-Squared. MC are his initials, see, and the "squared" comes from the fact that he's good at Maths. Max, another classmate and the most irritating guy in the whole school, joked that MC-Squared had gone for re-circumcision. Max always had silly things to say about everyone.

I was pleased when Yanda took MC's seat. I would have found it hard to cope through the day without her next to me.

I asked her if she liked rap and pointed out the lyrics that MC and I had copied onto the desk. The ones in the centre were my favourite. They were Eminem's, and they read:

I guess words are a motherfucker, they can be great
Or they can be great, or even worse, they can teach hate
It's like these kids hang on every single statement we make
Like they worship us, plus all the stores ship us platinum
Now how the fuck did this metamorphosis happen?

Yanda read the lyrics in silence.

'Yes, really now; how the hell did this metamorphosis happen?' she said. Her face transformed from happy to emotionless. Her head people seemed to drift away as she stared at the word her finger was pointing at: metamorphosis.

'How did my life metamorphose so suddenly?' she asked no one in particular. 'How did my life get so messed up and metaphorical? And what am I supposed to do with these metaphoric remains of what used to be me?'

Then, to my alarm, she dissolved into convulsive sobs. V-Nesh, her deskmate, who was also MC's girlfriend, helped me to get her to her feet, and we walked her out. Then V-Nesh and I stood and hugged her, trying to calm her down. Behind us, I heard the class bursting into laughter as Max invented crazy stories about the cause of Yanda's crying. They ranged from her being recently diagnosed with HIV, to having had her fifth abortion.

'Don't do it,' said V-Nesh, holding me back to stop me from going back inside the classroom. She'd read my intention to punch Max in the face and boot the bastard in the nuts.

There was this look in her brown eyes that told me she also knew the cause of Yanda's outburst. She probably did, since they'd been deskmates for nearly four months now.

I knew stuff about MC too. He'd told me some of his experiences at the mountain when he went in 1998. The ordeal of being cut and the difficulties of seclusion, and how much it all took out of you. It was discomforting information, for someone who was soon to go through it himself.

It was only later that I got to hear the reason for Yanda's crying outbreak. It was chaotic at our school that day. The usual schedule was interrupted by a visit from a group of AIDS activists, coming to talk to us about a variety of life skills topics, such as STDs, TB, safe abortions, domestic violence and substance abuse. While the rest of the school congregated in the school hall – which was really just two classrooms with the ceiling-board partition removed to make them into one large one – Yanda and I took the opportunity to abscond and have some private time together.

We sat side by side in our empty grade 12A classroom, and Yanda resumed the story of her life that she'd begun to try and tell me on the bus that morning; the unfolding of her metamorphosis, as she preferred to call it.

'You don't have to do this, really,' I said. I did not want her to start telling me things she was not ready to disclose.

'No, I do. I have to do this, today. You don't need to do anything, just listen. There are things I want you to know. Some of them, you're not going to like. There might even be a change of heart from your side when you've heard what I have to say. But I have to tell you.' She started to weep again.

In many ways, Yanda's story overlapped with my own. She was born in Cape Town and raised by her single mother. When she was fifteen they moved in with her stepfather into his double-storey house in Rosebank. Yanda was enrolled in a Model C school in Seapoint. At that time she was the only black student there. She was treated as special by everyone and she felt she was, too. She was doing well at school, getting good grades in class and playing lots of sport. Her English improved vastly.

She made friends with a girl called Tracey, who was tall and had blonde hair, and a sprinkle of brown dots below her eyes. Tracey's family were well-off, and she liked to do things that were adventurous.

She and Yanda started smoking *zol* together, and then they graduated to sniffing white powder, which Tracey knew how to acquire. It was the white powder that ruined both their lives. Before they knew it, they were addicted.

Yanda's schoolwork deteriorated and so did her health. The powder burnt her insides and she started throwing up after every meal. She lost weight dramatically and developed permanent dark patches under her eyes. More than once she collapsed in school. Her mother knew that something was going on and so did her teachers.

One day Yanda and Tracey were called into the principal's office and threatened with expulsion. It did no good. After numerous hearings and warnings, repeated almost daily, the two of them were expelled.

It was the middle of the school year and Yanda had nothing to do with her time. She reconnected with Tracey and they carried on where they'd left off. Things went from bad to worse, for by this time Yanda was hooked and needed to sustain her habit.

She started doing sex with strangers she met at the beachfront. She'd disappear from home for days and come back looking like the 15-year-old junkie she'd become. It was after the incident when she and Tracey were caught by the police, in possession of drugs, that her mother decided to send her to the villages to learn humanness anew.

At the end of that year her uncle, who was a teacher, decided to take guardianship of her on behalf of his sister. He enrolled her at a boarding school in Queenstown. Trouble followed her. She'd hardly been there a few months when she began to have run-ins with the school authorities. After she was expelled from residence, she moved in with her boyfriend, a minibus taxi driver. He paid her school fees and transported her to and from school. He also bought her powder and *weed*. She consumed them with the vigour with which they'd begun to consume her.

It was when her boyfriend kicked her out that Yanda finally woke up to what her life had become. After a particularly bad night of squatting in the boys' dorm, doing all six of them in turn, she decided that she had to turn her life around.

As soon as she'd finished her exams, she gathered enough money and boarded a minibus taxi to come and stay with her grandparents in Mbekweni. She discovered that she had once again conceived.

'I went to have it taken out. It was the fifth in two years,' she said, breaking down into sobs again.

I wanted to say something but I didn't know what. I held her and cuddled her, for she was shivering. There was a bull frog inside my Adam's apple. Despite everything that she'd just told me, I still loved her. Anyway, how could I judge her? Her story was not so different from mine in its essence. I'd also done things in my past that I wasn't proud of. The truth was, we were both lucky to have a second chance at life.

'I love you, Chris,' she said, still sobbing bitterly. 'I wish I could be with you but I can't. I'm evil. I'm dirty. There is blood dripping from my hands. I have scars inside and outside my body.' She held out her scabbed wrists for me to see. 'I'm sorry if I led you on. But I'm letting you go now; escape, while you have the chance. I will only bring misery into your life.'

I tried to change her mind. I told her I didn't care what her past was, and I meant it. I tried to explain that I also wasn't clean, that I'd come here for the same reason she had, to start my life over again. But she wasn't listening.

'I can't be with anyone. Don't you understand? Not now, not yet,' she said.

And that was the end of what had hardly even begun.

9

My grand plan had finally seemed complete when my love affair with Yanda had begun. But that was short-lived, and in terms of my love life I was right back where I started. I didn't let that distract me from my other goals, though. I was still intending to go for circumcision in December. My anxiety over this prospect was gaining momentum inside my skull. I suppose it was the nervousness experienced by every uncircumcised boy.

The thing I feared most of all was being cut. Damn, but that must be agonising, I thought. And what do they use, like, to slice the thing off? And how long does it take? Do they, like, chop fast? Or peel it away little by little, like? Are you supposed to watch while it's happening, or close your eyes? These were some of the questions buzzing around my head.

Before that event came to pass, however, I needed to achieve a university entry requirements in my finals. I dreaded the thought of having to go back to the life I once lived at e*kasi*. I wanted nothing even close to that kind of life. This became my main motivation to succeed. I was driven by the spectre of my past to study and study some more. My grades were coming along satisfactorily, but the proof of my efforts would be in the finals.

Even if I did not have Yanda as my girlfriend, I still had her as my friend, my best friend. After she'd calmed down that day, we'd been able to talk more about our situation. I'd

explained my own background to her and some of the things
that had brought me here. Although with reluctance on my
part, we'd agreed to allow each other some recovery time
from our previous lives. Yanda had told me she'd rather not
have me at all than have me and hurt me – or, worse, lose
me as a friend. She repeated that she needed to trust herself
first before she could open up to other people. So, a sexual
relationship between us at this time was not possible. But the
affection remained strong.

I lost the tracksuit top to her. She wore that oversized thing
practically every time I saw her. She didn't seem to care about
the clumsy look of it and asked me to hand over the bottoms
as well. It was my pleasure to do so.

We were very close. Being apart for any length of time was
difficult for both of us. On weekends I'd head for Mbekweni
village as soon as I finished milking the cows. We'd sit at the
Prices Dale bus shelter until her grandmother sent word for
her to come home. We kissed when we felt like it. But that's
all; kisses, nothing more. We'd postponed the acting-on-it
part indefinitely.

'What if you fell in love with someone else, would you have
the guts to tell me?' Yanda surprised me by asking out of
the blue one day. I answered 'Yes', but I suspected then that
something was up and feared I was about to lose her, that
she'd found someone else. I wish I could say I was wrong, but
I wasn't.

During those wintry days, Max befriended Yanda. It was
clear something was going on between them. He'd buy her
lollipops and other things, have endless conversations with
her outside the classroom. Once, they walked into class
holding hands. I'd searched for wisdom from MC-Squared's
eyes. He'd shrugged his shoulders at me.

The next day, Yanda didn't bring her books for me to pack
into my satchel as usual. She hugged them to her in the old
way, walking side by side with Max. When I recovered from

the shock, I was met with V-Nesh's knowing eyes. She shook her head and pulled the tail of her new cornrows.

There was no trace of Yanda at the bus shelter that afternoon and for the first time in ages I boarded the bus alone. It felt all wrong, empty and lonely. The head people whispered consolations to me, but the chest people didn't believe them.

It was disorientating when the bus did not stop at the Prices Dale bus shelter. I saw Yanda's grandmother and Days turn away with a drooped back. Ten minutes later I got off as usual at my graveyard stop. When my eyes landed on the familiar landmark of the huge twin breasts, they looked tired and weathered to me. I found nothing arousing about their bareness today.

The dogs came running to meet me as they usually did, but I warned them not to jump on me. Reading my mood, they tucked their tails between their legs and ran for cover.

I found it difficult to fall asleep that night. There was an annoying *kwak kwak* of courting bull frogs from the river. The sky was moonless and dark, a true reflection of the feelings of the chest people.

I woke to a bleak morning of biting frost. The bus came late, and everything felt wrong. The crow journalists were working overtime, carrying their bad news between graveyard and church and back again. We'd been roused in the early hours by the disturbing sound of the knell ringing its doom. I learnt later that it rang for *Oom* Dan's wife, Kholiswa. Long weakened by her stroke, she hadn't woken up that morning. Her loss was wrenching, for, like *Oom* Dan, she was well-liked and respected by all. There was a mournful atmosphere in the village the whole of that day.

Things did not get any better as the day advanced. There was no Yanda running for the bus at Prices Dale, no grandmother or Days to be seen on the red *stoep*. The back-seat *kaka* boys were at their noisiest and most annoying.

I found Yanda sitting in the empty classroom, scribbling

away at her Maths homework. It was the first time I had known her not to have done it. I added one plus one and found what it equalled: Yanda had slept at Yonda last night. Not at V-Nesh's, not anywhere else but at Max's.

My attempts to make eye contact with her were to no avail. She stared into nothingness and I couldn't read the expression on her face. I wished she would just say something to me, instead of leaving me hanging with her loud speechlessness.

It wasn't until lunch time that we spoke. I'd pulled a chair outside and was sitting there enjoying the gentle sunshine while I re-read the story of Pius Ndawula, the loyal custodian of King Sabalangira's tomb. I looked up from my reading and saw her walking by with Max in the direction of the store.

Ten minutes later she came back again, this time walking alone. I glanced at her and saw guilt, anger and disappointment in her face; the head people told me there were suicidal thoughts as well. It turned out they weren't wrong, the head people. The chest people began to thud faster as I realised she was coming up to me. I threw my head back, looking up at the sky, trying to hold back the tears from falling. Yanda walked into the classroom and brought out another chair, which she placed next to mine. She sat down, biting her lips.

'What are you reading?' she asked.

'Pius Ndawula,' I told her. It was one of the popular stories doing the rounds that we'd read together and discussed over and over.

We sat without talking, our head people full of words but our mouths not knowing what to say. Finally, Yanda said:

'Did you eat something?'

'Not hungry... you?'

'Nah.'

There was silence again.

I suppose she was still busy thinking of a better way of softening my defences. What she did not realise was that these arms were wide open. I looked at her and it was hard to say whose eyes were glassier, mine or hers.

'I don't want to hear it,' I told her.

'But you're mad at me?'

'I wish I was.'

It was at this point that we were interrupted by someone approaching from the direction of the staffroom. She wasn't one of the learners but an older girl whom I didn't recognise at all. She had very pale skin and lots of make-up on her face. Her relaxed red hair was as chaotic as tree branches. I found out later that she was Max's girlfriend.

'Hello,' she greeted. I could see her nose widening and narrowing as she spoke.

'Hello, *sisi*,' I replied.

'Can I have a word with you... Yanda?' she asked, her eyes about to pop out of their sockets.

Tensed, Yanda eyed me. She gave me that look that excludes everyone else and leaves only the two of us in the world. Then she stood up. The red-haired girl was busy cracking her knuckles. It was as if she could not wait to lay her big hands on Yanda's body.

'Well, you can have your word some other time. Yanda and I are in the middle of something right now... if you will excuse us,' was what came out of my mouth. I had not planned it. It simply came out like a long-held fart. I saw Yanda fall back into her chair with relief. The red-haired girl looked at me as if she was about to strew me with the bile that I imagined had begun to yellow her tongue.

'Your little boyfriend won't be here after school. I will show you then, you slut,' she said in deep vernacular, and marched away at speed. I knew that if I hadn't been there, if I hadn't farted those words, Yanda would have been made dough. I caught sight of *la way* wagging her accusing finger at us through the staffroom window. This time I knew I saw it, I wasn't imagining things. *What's wrong with her?* I wondered.

'Why did you do that?' Yanda asked. The question disappointed me. Yanda wasn't a person who asked me "why". She always knew the goings-on of the head people without asking. Or had she forgotten, overnight?

'I wish I knew,' I replied.

After school we walked towards the bus stop, everyone staring to see us together again. I hated the way people looked at my Yanda. There was something unpalatable in their accusatory stares.

On the bus home, we sat next to each other as usual and I got off at the Prices Dale bus stop with Yanda. I was scared I was not going to see her again. The way she'd kept so quiet on the journey made me anxious. I kept remembering the scars on her wrists and I wanted to tell her not to do stupid things. But I also did not want to import thoughts into her head if they were not there already. I wrestled with this until we got to Prices Dale, without resolving what to say to her that would ensure she would still be alive the following day.

'I missed you,' I finally said.

'C'mon, even Satan knows that!' she replied, and laughed for the first time.

Her laughter reassured me.

'I'm glad you're yourself again,' I said. 'I was worried about you... that I'd lost you.'

'I'm sorry,' she replied.

At this point Days arrived, his tail wagging in greeting. I saw her grandmother take her place on the *stoep*. Everything was back the way it was supposed to be.

'Friends?' I asked, holding my hand out. She took it and squeezed my fingers.

'Yes. Friends for now. Lovers for the future. And parents in the making. Isn't it, Days? Isn't it?' she said, bending to brush the dog between its erect ears, as if to say "sorry" to him, too.

'Well, I think Days missed you. Go have a good time with him. Call me if he refuses to leave the bathroom,' I joked.

'You call me tonight. Will you, Chris? Please, please, please.'

'Okay,' I said, 'I will.'

We kissed goodbye and I continued on my way, my feet barely touching the ground. It was a long way to walk but I didn't mind that. I think I broke several athletic records that day as I sprang, jumped, dribbled and punched the frosty air all the way home.

10

And then before I knew it, it was November and Item One on my grand plan was just around the corner. MC-Squared was thrilled that I was now going to join him in the circumcision ranks. It was long overdue. We would at last be able to talk the same language: the language of manhood.

He began outlining the procedure to me, explaining the objectives of the whole thing and clearing out some of the mysteries around the process. He told me I was expected to observe, listen and act.

'You must look at everything. Observation is vital, especially during the crucial time of the aftercare,' he emphasised. 'You must listen with all your hair follicles when you're being instructed. Pay attention to the language that is used. It is the manhood language that you will be expected to use later to explain yourself to others. And you must be able to take actions to heal yourself, to know how to use the traditional remedies. So: observe, listen and act; that is your journey into manhood.'

Then he went on to clarify things about the eight days of seclusion in more detail. He told me what I was to look out for, what I was expected to do, and how things were meant to look at the different stages. All of the things MC-Squared was telling me was prohibited information. I wasn't a man yet, and I had no business knowing manhood things. I couldn't guess how vital his disclosures would turn out to be, and how grateful I would be for them in the ordeal to come. For they would be the only guidance I could rely on.

The circumcision process is a physical and tangible manifestation of what manhood is really about. It teaches you how to endure, how to manoeuvre your way through and out of the difficult situations that life presents to you. It trains you in the lessons of patience, for it is something that cannot be rushed through but can only be completed step by step. That is some of what MC-Squared explained to me.

He also lectured me on the crucial terminology and its appropriate use, the code language that is shared between men and must be used by initiates at the mountain. 'You might do everything right and come out healed but you remain a boy if you cannot articulate your manhood,' he told me.

'Everything means something in this world. There are many ways of becoming a man, but each and every man has the responsibility to articulate his way into manhood. By that I mean, you can't tell us you are a man simply because you don't have a foreskin, or because we were there when you were circumcised. There are many people who don't have foreskins and whose ceremonies we attended but they are still not men, you see. Our process is orderly, and it is this orderly process, which begins the minute you declare yourself a man that you need to gain eloquence in articulating. Not only must you understand manhood as a concept but you need to experience it, you see. And you have to carry it through from start to end – meaning from the minute you are circumcised to your last breath in this life. There are no short cuts or bypasses. It is a winding and thorny road that you embark on. This journey is about crossing rivers. This is your first one. Next, you'll be taking a wife, raising children, building a home, and those are the rivers lying ahead of you until you cross the last one, which is your death.'

Finally, he told me the things I was to avoid. Above all the cautions, MC-Squared emphasised that I should avoid ending up in hospital at all costs.

'It is better to die than to go to hospital. It would be the end of you anyway,' he warned me. 'There's no living space for failed men in our society. Either you become a man the expected way, or you are no one at all.'

Discussions about my forthcoming circumcision were less intense, but no less satisfying with Yanda. She was as excited as if it was she who was to be made a man. She promised she'd visit me after my seclusion. We'd watch the sunsets together, we'd stroll at the Ox-Kraal bladder, enjoying the smoothness of sand beneath our feet.

She even offered to make the invitation cards for my coming-out ceremony, which we estimated would be exactly four weeks after my going to the mountain. She'd buy me a huge *Dobs* hat as a present, and we'd stay together all through the night of the ceremony.

'After that we'll be heading off to Wits University to start our new lives,' she said. You see, Yanda had a grand plan of her own, which had me as its anchor. Just as mine had her as its anchor. The difference was that her planning went down to the last detail.

'Why Wits?' I asked, still digesting my pleased surprise to learn that she'd decided her future and mine lay together.

'Instead of where, exactly?'

'Well... UCT, for instance.'

'Haven't you had enough of Cape Town?' she threw at me. 'I have. No, Wits is a clean start for both of us.'

I saw the sense in what she said. Gauteng would be the clean slate we both needed. There was no way we wanted to go back and drown ourselves in the place of our former doom. We'd both worked hard to change things for ourselves, and we weren't keen to put our lives on rewind.

Our village colleagues had accepted us as fellow travellers in the movie called life, not *kasi* rejects chased out by the

harshness of the city. You could say we had been de-kasi-fied,
if you like.

We were true rural bumpkins now. We no longer held
ourselves aloof from those around us, or needed drugs to get
us through the day. We'd become what our city friends would
have categorised as "softies". Our joy lay in simple things:
the greenness of sowing fields, the thorniness of bush, the
shape of mountains, the gayness of dogs, the pureness of the
atmosphere and freedom from toxins, speed and noise.

I couldn't imagine breaking into another person's house,
tearing their mattresses apart, emptying their drawers and
wardrobes, and sometimes their refrigerators, too. I no longer
had in me the readiness to kill if it came to the crunch. And
I was no longer looking at cars to check if they had *umgqala-
gqala*.

I think both Yanda and I had reached that important stage
where we could laugh about our past. You see, that is the
time you can consider yourself healed, if you are able to laugh
about your pain, and tell your story without feeling angry or
defensive.

It had taken a while but Yanda, my dear Yanda, had
finally acted upon one of my suggestions. Once, when she'd
confessed to me that she was still haunted by visions of the
five she'd bled away, and how difficult she found it to let go
of that pain, I'd suggested to her that she should name the
aborted ones, and welcome them into her life, instead of
imagining them as wasted souls. I'd said she should celebrate
their birthdays, and then let them go.

'Zizo, Zonke, Zona, Izono, Zam,' she'd said, and smiled.

'What do you mean "These Are All Sins Of My Own"?' I'd
asked in confusion.

'Their names,' she said.

I engulfed her in a wordless hug for a longer time than
usual. I understood that those were the names she had given
to the late five. It was a declaration of acceptance, and not

a disclaimer. In naming the five, she was owning up to her responsibility in making them. I liked that. It meant that she was able to redefine herself beyond her previous experiences. She wasn't the whore who couldn't "keep them parallel", the way she'd thought of herself. She was just a young woman who'd had a rough teenagehood.

11

December soon came. While our examination scripts were being marked somewhere in the Eastern Cape by strangers, I was busy doing the last preparations for my circumcision ceremony. I had climbed the mountain's right-hand breast to axe trees for firewood that could be used by those at home during the time of my absence. The wood would also be put to use during my going-in ceremony, as well as the much-anticipated feast on my coming out.

The trees were wet and heavy, for it had been raining without a pause. The long hours of hacking with the axe brought up blisters on my soft palms and the hauling of the heavy branches from the breast down to our house caused them to burst and the skin to peel away. I welcomed the pain. This, I thought with pleasure, was the beginning of my journey into manhood. Since endurance was an integral part of that process, I might as well get used to tolerating physical pain. The chopping, hauling and stacking of the firewood was a gesture from my side that I was ready, that I could initiate things and carry them through to the end on my own, without the intervention of grown-ups.

Grandmother ululated and danced as I descended with the wet branches one by one. She was joined by the neighbours. They all knew what she was ululating about, and everyone was excited and jubilant. It filled me with pride to see the mothers of my mother celebrating on my behalf. They invented songs featuring my name as they went in and out of their houses, doing routine errands. Let me tell you, that ululation, those songs, stay with you forever. They resound among your head people and echo between your ears for a long, long time. I can still recall them even today. They remind me of the unfulfilled hopes that Mother, Grandmother, our neighbours and I all had that I would become a man the expected way.

We were all wrong.

When I mention neighbours, I include *Bra*'Mtyobo, who was our closest neighbour. He had this fantastic whistle that he could play like a jazz instrument, as if it was coming out of a horn instead of just his mouth. Sometimes, in the middle of the night it drove me mad, for its shrill, disjointed notes had the sound of meaningless insanity.

On this occasion, however, *Bra*'Mtyobo's whistle was not the jazzy vibrato that I disliked so much but a skilful and melodic rendition of *Somagwaza*, the traditional song that is sung during rite of passage ceremonies. It went something like this:

> *Hhe Somagwaza ngizoyigwaza lenkwenkwe*
> *Hha yoh weh, iyoh-hoho*
> *Hha yoh weh, Somagwaza...*

The song takes the form of a warning given by a traditional surgeon to the mysterious Somagwaza that he is going to stab "this boy" with his assegai, right now. He tells Somagwaza that the cowardly boys have all chickened out, but this one, this boy here, will be stabbed at once. It sent shivers down my back just to think about that momentous stab.

Somagwaza was held to be the first man ever to be circumcised the proper way, a long time ago. He'd actually stone-cised himself.

He'd laid a stone between his legs, pulled the foreskin over it and pounded the damn thing with another pointy stone until it fell away. He'd then used certain leaves and herbs to nurse his circumcision back to health, and he emerged a man. Somagwaza became a god amongst men.

We, the uninitiated, didn't know the truthfulness of this story but it was believable and scary. We were just boys, after all, and whatever came our way was gospel truth.

*Bra'*Mtyobo wasn't looking at me as he ballooned his cheeks and whistled *Somagwaza*. He was going about his daily wall-painting job, trying to finish the word "PALAMENT" that he was busy painting on the face of his house. In the past, he'd written "SABC STYUDO" above the front door, and then changed it to "BIN LADEN" a few weeks later. This had brought about a fierce argument between him and my uncle. Uncle objected to *Bra'*Mtyobo glorifying the names of "terrorists". It had been fine when *Bra'*Mtyobo had written "Mugabe", "Mandela" and "Nyerere", but not "Bin Laden". It had even been amusing when he'd painted De Klerk's bald head and stabbed it with an arrow. What was *Bra'*Mtyobo now trying to tell the people about us, that we were hiding Bin Laden in our village? Did this *rakie* called *Bra'*Mtyobo not know that the whole world was searching for this Bin Laden person? Didn't he know what Bin Laden had done? Uncle had been really upset and he and *Bra'*Mtyobo had got into a heated argument. It wasn't funny. Grandfather had had to intervene. In the end, *Bra'*Mtyobo had smeared paint over the words "Bin Laden" and left it to dry, and after that the front wall had stayed for a long time without a word on its face.

Today as I hauled my trees home and saw *Bra'*Mtyobo painting his misspelled "Parliament" on the wall in red paint, I wondered what uncle would make of it when he returned from his sheep-shearing. It was hard to see how he could start an argument with His Excellency *Bra'*Mtyobo about "Parliament". But you never knew with those two. As much as it is impossible to keep two bulls in the same kraal without bloodshed, so it is equally so keeping two psychos as neighbours without fights erupting over their various hallucinations.

When the firewood pile was high enough, I brought my axe down from the mountain and rested it. The next step was to visit the Sada clinic for a blood test. They were going to test me for HIV and whatever else it is they test for in the blood of prospective initiates. Yes, me, getting HIV tested! I was cool about it, though. The knowledge that I hadn't yet parted ways with my innocence settled any fears I might have had. I knew HIV wasn't malaria, that you don't get it from a mosquito bite, and neither do you get it by kissing. I was safe, I was pretty sure of that.

All the same, I felt I needed a counselling session with my Yanda about it. At that time we shared everything. As it was, three long days had passed without me seeing her, and I was having withdrawal symptoms.

We sat at Prices Dale, scanning each other as if we'd been apart for months and catching up on each other's news. She told me she'd received provisional acceptance letters from Wits for both of us, but she'd forgotten to bring them to show me. Yes, true to her word, Yanda had applied to Wits for the two of us. We'd decided it was better if she attended to the academic matters since I had other important things on my mind. She did not want any slip-ups that might result in us not being together next year. She told me that Wits was going to send our final admission letters as soon as our results came out, which would coincide with my coming out from the mountain. Then we would be off to Gauteng together. We were certain we would both achieve university passes. There was not even the slightest doubt in our minds about that.

'Let's just say Satan pulled a fast one and you and I didn't pass, tell me then, who would?' she'd said.

'No one,' I'd agreed.

On my side, I hadn't much news to share, other than *Bra*'Mtyobo's recent bout of painting. Yanda burst into fits of laughter at my story. It was good to see her laughing so much. I wish I'd known it was the last time I'd hear that laugh of hers.

I told her about the blood test, pretending I was worried about the HIV thing. She reacted as expected, by laughing at me. Then she said I mustn't rush for it, since I would get the HI-virus in due course.

'But for now,' she joked, 'we know that you're so clean I could drink your blood.'

It was a stupid joke and I'd let her know it.

My HIV test at the clinic gave the predicted negative result. Even though I'd been expecting it, I couldn't help feeling relieved. The way was now clear for me to be issued with my licence to be circumcised. The nurse first wanted to know who was going to circumcise me. I told her it was Gecangotolo. He was well known at the clinic and held to be a respected traditional surgeon. This brought some relief to me. I'd been dreading to be circumcised by somebody who was inexperienced. Horrible stuff was reported about these fly-by-night surgeons, ranging from the surgical errors they had committed, to performing under the influence of alcohol. If he was well known at the clinic, I could rest assured that this Geca was a reputable surgeon in circumcision ranks.

The clinic nurse asked me who my attendant would be and I told her it was my uncle. This wasn't official yet, but I suspected it was going to be him who would be assigned to supervise me during my seclusion. I presumed that he was the only person Grandfather would trust enough to ascribe the traditional attendant's responsibility to. Things didn't turn out the way I anticipated in that regard, either.

I was then told that a male nurse would visit my hut once every week during my stay on the mountain. I was surprised and a little dismayed by this information. Since when were medical people allowed at the mountain? I was told that this was a recent decision by the Circumcision Task Team commissioned by the Provincial Department of Health. The purpose of the visits was to try and reduce the rate of morbidity and mortality due to septic circumcision. The male nurse, who would preferably be a circumcised man himself, would determine if things could be handled the traditional way or if medical intervention was needed. In the event of the latter possibility, he would decide whether things could be settled medically at the mountain or if hospitalisation was needed.

'It's a progressive move,' the nurse added.

I wasn't sure I approved. It sounded to me like an unwanted intrusion into the culture of our forefathers, and I was troubled by the idea. What would people think when they saw a male nurse coming out of my hut with a first-aid kit? I mean, that thing about septic circumcision only happened to people who did not do things the proper way, didn't it? Those were initiates who took drugs, had sex on the eve of circumcision, slept or drank water when they were not supposed to, and generally didn't follow protocol. These things that stained our customs were, in any case, happening on the other side, in regions such as Transkei, where they circumcised twelve-year olds. Not in our villages, where we did things properly. As far as I knew, there hadn't been any cases of people landing up in hospital from the villages in our area, and I wasn't planning to be the one to change that. I was confident that we were immune from this septic circumcision scourge.

Once again, I was wrong. I could not know that a nurse's visit was something I would spend my days at the mountain praying for.

12

___

It was my last night as one of the boys and we were holding an all-night vigil, a farewell to me as a boy. The night was far advanced, and I was desperate to sleep. I'd been begging for hours to be allowed to go and lie down, knowing that I wouldn't have the chance again for the next eight days. But my companions refused to let me leave my own vigil. They were afraid that I might run away, and they'd be held responsible. Surprisingly, escape was the last thing on my mind.

I just needed to sleep.

'Please, *majita*,' I begged them again.

It was agreed that I should be guarded while I slept by two of the boys. The appointed guards were given a tin can full of beer and left to keep watch over me in my room. I drifted off to sleep and left them to their talk of witches and women and their various masturbation episodes. Their sexual experiences weren't very different from mine, I realised in my drowsiness.

It felt like I'd only been asleep for five minutes when Uncle came knocking at my bedroom door. I felt something hit me on the shin and I jumped to life. It was KG, one of my guard boys, hitting me in farewell. KG and I had grown up together, shepherding Grandfather's sheep, before I left for my father's place in Cape Town. When I came back, we were still friends. That hit on the shin was the equivalent of a hug goodbye from him.

My black and white television set was playing a hit song by

the group called Trompies. It was the track *Fohloza*. I sang
along nervously while I put my soon-to-be-discarded pants on,
leaving the underwear off. It was the last time I would wear
these "boys" clothes. When I came back as a man, everything
I owned would be new. I was glad of the music to distract me
as I dressed.

Fohloza Fohloza Fohloza
Gao le monate le mpitseng
Gao le monate le mpitseng
Fohloza Fohloza Fohloza.

Fohloza is a catchy Sotho dance tune about the voluptuousness
of women in a dance hall, the way they move their big sexy
bodies as they dance. The song goes: 'When it's nice and
vibey and funky, please call me so that I can *fohloza*.'

Ta'Yongs' white Isuzu van was waiting outside the house to
take us to Sada township. He was my mother's cousin from
Cape Town, home for the December holidays. He had come
to transport us to the place where I would be circumcised.
As Uncle and I boarded the white van, I was surprised by my
grandfather's absence. I had expected him to be coming with
us. As the elder, he should have been there to ensure things
were done in the proper way.

There was very little talk as we drove. The time must have
been around 4am and it was still dark outside. But I could see
the amber and purple growing behind the mountain's boobs,
showing that dawn was on its way. The grass was soaked with
dew and the cocks were crowing to each other. I listened
to them for the last time as a boy, imagining the familiar
conversation between them:

Ndikhumbul'eDushe
Hamba siye
Andinabhulukhwe
Oh kulungile.

Their conversation related to the tale my mother used to tell me.

"Dushe" was the fabled place where chickens used to stay with the other birds, until they lost the keys to the safe that the hawk had given them.

Then they were kicked out from that place and forced to live as they do here on earth. That's why you see them scratching the ground, still hoping to find the lost keys and go back to Dushe. Meanwhile, hawk continues to punish them, coming to prey on the little chickens.

It was light by the time we got to Sada township. As we pulled up at Geca's place I was surprised – no, shocked – when he jumped out of *umdlongolo* mounted on top of big rocks beside his *veza* house. He was wearing a blue overcoat, but that was all I saw. Uncle warned me not to look lest I took fright at Geca's face. I heard him hop onto the back of our van as I stared at my now shaky knees. *Ta'*Yongs drove out of Sada and suddenly stopped the van in the middle of nowhere. I heard Geca jump down. Then *Ta'*Yongs and Uncle erupted into laughter and I was forced to look up. Geca was running off with the speed of a fifteen-year-old. I was confused by all of it.

'He has finished with you, *mtshana*,' Uncle said.

'You mean...' I was beginning to say, when *Ta'*Yongs ignited the engine and we drove on, following in the footsteps of Geca who by now had run to the river. I did not understand what they meant when they said he was finished with me. It couldn't be that the cutting was done?

'Check yourself, you are a man now,' *Ta'*Yongs said.

'Go on, check yourself,' Uncle encouraged.

I opened my fly and peeped through it. There was just the usual darkness inside.

'Take it out and look at it, *mtshana*,' Uncle said.

I felt something, now that I'd been alerted to it. There were little throbs right at the fore of the head. I inserted my hand into my genitals and cupped my limb. It felt heavier than usual, and there was this moistness.

'Careful, careful, *mtshana*,' one of my companions said.

My face must have turned into a grimace as I pulled the limb out, not wanting to mess things up. I didn't know for sure how it would look or what had been done, you know. I was expecting to see a wounded limb that dripped blood all around. Uncle and *Ta*'Yongs burst into helpless laughter, that "gotcha" kind of laughter, as I inspected my uncut limb. Shit! I thought. They'd been playing the fool with me, and I'd fallen for it. I would learn that this hide and seek business was the way things were done in this new world.

Ta'Yongs parked the car and we walked towards the river. The summer dew had soaked the long grass and our shoes and trousers were soon wet from it. When we got to the riverbank, *Ta*'Yongs explained that "observe, listen and act" thing that I'd already been told by MC-Squared. I nodded as though I was hearing it for the first time.

There was the gentle whisper of waters as the river chased itself. Surprisingly, Geca was not there. If ever there was a time when I didn't know whether I was dreaming or if things were real, it was that morning. Where the fuck was this Geca?

I took off my clothes and Uncle sat me down. He and *Ta*'Yongs threw river water over me, to raise the gooseflesh that would help to numb my skin. Then we waited for what seemed like seven hours, according to the head people's clock. I don't know what happened next, but suddenly Geca was there, emerging right in front of me from nowhere. He did not say much. He widened my legs with his bony knees. Held my limb in a way so awkward I couldn't recognise it as my own flesh. Then he head-butted me on the chin and I bit my tongue. *What the hell?!*

I looked at Uncle for help. He motioned with his fingers that I should observe. I ducked my head past Geca's and peeped through the gap. Shit! It was so quick I couldn't even describe what I saw. I'd missed the first crucial observation. The one that followed was disgusting, especially for someone who doesn't like the sight of wounds. I was then ordered to declare myself a man and I tried. By the way, this is funny because I wouldn't be asked to undeclare myself later, when I did not make it. Anyway, there was a bull frog on my Adam's apple, and the declaration came out like a forced "*kwaak*".

Me, a man, just like that? I thought.

Geca began tightening the leather strip that he had wrapped around my limb. It left me feeling numb. He emerged from between my legs and I looked into his face for the first time. My uncle was right, he did look scary, that Geca. He had a lot of folds in his face, and he was all sweaty from his exertion.

He went to wash his hands while I was ordered to put my pants back on. It seemed impracticable, what with this thonged thing so stubbornly vertical. It was like I was being asked to wear my school trousers with my morning hardness fully erect, an impossible manoeuvre. But, hey, a man's got to do what a man's got to do, ain't that right?

We drove off to the village. Geca refused a lift back to his house; he had a job to go to. He hopped away like a calf, jumping and running as if celebrating the damage he'd just caused me. I felt my heart pounding right through my limb, thud, thud, thud. There was no pain yet, just numbness, and a warmness between my thighs. Whatever happened now, there was no turning back.

The mountain's boobs looked thornier than ever before. I fantasised that they would just fall on top of us, murder everyone with their thorns. Our blood would flood into the furrow that wound through our village down to Ox-Kraal bladder. The bladder would be so full it would menstruate our blood down to Queenstown, where farmers would drain it to sprinkle onto their crops. Then there would be no circumcision any longer, since we would all have bled to death. The soreness that was beginning to grip me made me wish that something like that could actually happen.

13

It turned out that Grandfather was so drunk he could not attend my going to the mountain. While the boys had held their all-night vigil to see me off into manhood, Grandfather had been doing a different kind of vigil in his bedroom. It was the first time I had heard of such a thing, that the grandfather of the initiate is so drunk he can't be present. The person responsible for ensuring my smooth transition into manhood was incapable. So *Oom* Dan took it upon himself to oversee things. We were still pondering over the absence of my grandfather when a white van turned into the village. It had come to collect Uncle and the other shearers, who were needed to go and shear a farmer's flock in Kamastone. Uncle ran to fetch his shearing scissors, and off they went.

I understand that in some ways Uncle had no choice. When you were summoned to a shearing job, you had to go. If you turned down that opportunity you might not get another one. And besides, he needed the money. But it left me stranded, with no one to be my attendant.

It was *Oom* Dan and *Ta'*Yongs who helped me make my own hut in the mountain. The temporary hut should be made early in the morning by the village men. It was Grandfather's role to host the men at his kraal and preside over the preparations for my time at the mountain. But when we got back to the village from Sada, we found that nothing had been done, and the only man present was *Oom* Dan. The sight of him standing there alone confused me. I can still picture him in his blazer and black pants, leaning on his knobkerrie, with his hat of woven plastic. I learnt later that the reason the other men had stayed away was because my grandfather had instructed that no stray man must be found meddling in any of the business of my circumcision; his son, my uncle, was going to take care of things. But where was that trusted son of his now? The same absent place that he was himself. That was my grandfather's contribution to my circumcision – his absence. He didn't even bother to examine the extent of my surgery.

The three of us, *Oom* Dan, *Ta'*Yongs and I, dug holes and inserted poles right at the tip of the cleavage in the mountain. The hut was a diagonal structure, built of zinc sheets, with a door of sacking. More sacks were stuffed into the corners to keep the cold wind out. *Oom* Dan whined to himself now and again as he worked.

'This, my *sbali, nc nc nc,*' he moaned, shaking his head in disapproval.

*Ta'*Yongs helped me down onto my white blanket with the red stripes, and smeared my face with the mud he'd made from an anthill. There was no water in that place, and I don't know how he could possibly have made such soft mud. It was one more mystery in a day of mysteries.

I began to feel the mud draining the moisture out of my face. *Ta'* Yongs then allowed me to practise the thong bandaging technique several times before he left me. He said I was already doing it better than he'd done it on his third day. I was flattered; it seemed that MC-Squared's advice about observation had come in handy. That was the last time I saw *Ta'*Yongs until the day of my coming out.

Oom Dan climbed the mountain to search for the herbs and other things I was going to need. It was wrong that he, at his age, should have to do this – a job meant for attendants. But where was my attendant? He was Attendant-Gone-Sheep-Shearing.

I began to observe things: there is my axe. Here is my stick. There is the small lamp that *Ta'*Yongs has just made for me out of a tin filled with paraffin. He also put those eight rocks around the fireplace in the middle of my hut. He said I was to get rid of one each day to keep myself orientated. Okay, so that is that. And the hut is facing east. And there is that hole, I forget what *Ta'*Yongs said it was for. *Shit!* I thought.

I ventured to do the aftercare procedure, unwrapping the thong and rewrapping it again. *Ta'*Yongs had instructed that I repeat it every fifth minute. If I did that, he said, the wound would heal nicely, and I should be a man in four days. With those words echoing among the head people, the possibility of being a man in just four days, I vowed to myself that I would work hard at doing things the way I'd been told. I didn't need any fucking attendant after all.

I got the thong thing right, although I mishandled it at first. I gripped and gripped and rolled tight until the thong assumed its necessary erectness. Good stuff. I told myself that this evil drowsiness that was beginning to lull me had better return to its handler, since I wasn't going to entertain it. My business there did not involve sleeping.

I repeated this delicate exercise of unwrapping and rewrapping until I noticed progress in the circumcision. I was impressed with myself. I was doing really well, despite Satan's will.

Oom Dan came back. He'd dug out some of the white clay stones from the mountain side. I knew the clay was made from rubbing the white rocks together until they become powder and then you add water to make a muddy paste. He also produced a mixture of greens and sat down, watching me repeat the dressing with my thong at estimated five-minute intervals while he separated the useful parts from the garbage in his greens. He then began to show me how I was to start using the herbs as soon as I observed a certain level of dryness in my limb. He let me try it a few times before he declared me a master. Again, I was flattered, what with all these compliments being thrown at me in one day.

It was about then that my ten-year-old brother came in, bringing me a tinful of maize grains that had been dipped in boiling water for about two seconds before they were left to dry and then served to me. I chewed a handful and spat it out in protest. How the hell was I expected to eat raw maize grains and still come out of that place alive? *Oom* Dan gave me a look that said this-is-the-manhood-you-said-you-wanted, deal-with-it. I dealt with my grains because I was hungry. It was midday already and I'd had nothing to eat since the previous night.

Oom Dan surveyed the inside of the hut, checking that I had all my basic necessities. He ordered my brother to bring more sacks to stuff into the corners lest the breeze should find its way in and make me sick. He also instructed him to bring a spade to dig a furrow that would steer water away from the hut if it rained. 'Don't bring any water here, you hear?' Dan told my brother.

'Don't send messages to your mothers. Don't bring your sisters to this place. Always wash your hands at the river when you come from here. What happens at the mountain stays at the mountain. *Izigqwathe* have no business in this place. Do we understand each other?' *Izigqwathe* is the code word for women. Literally, it means "snots".

'Make fire for this initiate at his request,' Dan went on. 'There must always be white clay here, and this initiate mustn't be as he is now. He must be white, like the goat he is supposed to be.' My brother nodded and chuckled at my supposed goatness.

He was then shown a handful of the herbs and told that, should our uncle not come back by tomorrow, he, my young brother, would have to climb the mountain every day of my seclusion, searching for these herbs. He was told where he could find them in abundance. As an afterthought, he was ordered to chain a dog at the mouth of the hut, lest baboons visited en masse.

I felt sorry for my brother. He was so young. How was he supposed to travel into the mountains alone with snakes and everything out there? What if those people who stole our sheep from the mountains should catch and murder him? It wasn't fair that one so young should be burdened with so much responsibility. I felt a tear making its way to the surface of my eye. I love my little brother. Very much. I reminded myself that a man does not cry.

My brother stared at me with concern. Then he had to go. It hurt me when he said his goodbyes.

'I will come back, *mkhwetha*,' he added, fighting his own tears but trying to reassure me at the same time. When I was ten, I wasn't half as brave as him.

It must have been just a few minutes after *Oom* Dan had left when I heard a voice I identified as my brother's at the mouth of the hut.

'Can I enter, *mkhwetha*?' he enquired.

'Yes,' I replied and quickly covered myself with the blanket, allowing only my mud-smeared face to appear. Boys are not supposed to see these things. There's no point in terrifying them ahead of time.

He pushed the sacking door aside and crawled inside. He was so small and vulnerable to me. I'd been his age, also ten, when Uncle went to the mountain. I'd also had to run his errands. But times were different then. For one thing, Uncle had his attendant. And he had been well cared for. Even though he had stolen off to be circumcised without permission, Grandfather had shown the proper concern for him and done his duty the way he was supposed to.

I was there at the house when the news came that Uncle and his friend, Afrika, had been discovered at Afrika's house, where they'd taken refuge after being circumcised. It was me who had to transport the zinc sheets on my head on a windy July morning to the mountain. My uncle's own uncle was allocated as his attendant, and I was ordered to run errands for him. I remembered how Grandfather, forgetting my presence, had pulled out his penis and showed it to *mkhwetha*, my uncle.

'This is how it must be at the end, you hear? Work, my son.'

But where was he now, my grandfather? And where was his son, my uncle, that I ran errands for all those years ago? Was my circumcision any different to theirs? Had my limb not also been cut?

My brother sat staring at the ground while my head people ran back along memory lane. I wanted to ask him what the matter was, and why he had hidden away until after Dan was gone. But I already saw the answer in his face. He was weeping. I had never before witnessed my brother sob so. It hurt to know that it was out of concern for me. He seemed to be the only person who cared. But there was little he could do to help.

Now he calmed down and told me that Mother had phoned from her school in the Transkei to find out how I was doing. She had not been able to attend my going-in ceremony because they were busy marking exam scripts. Her absence was understandable, and we had talked about this possibility in advance. She'd told me that I must pray in my every minute of doubt and difficulty, and she would do the same. My brother also passed on greetings from my eight-year-old sister.

I asked him if there was anyone else who had called, like, asking about me. His answer was 'No'.

There was silence.

'We're finished with exams now, so I'm not going to school anymore,' my brother declared. I took it that he was saying he would not leave me alone in this place. I had to work hard to persuade him that he should go back to school.

'Should I bring you more blankets?' he then asked me.

Clearly, my brother was stressing too much about the situation. He was set on bringing the whole bedroom up the mountain for my comfort. I had to be firm with him. I assured him again that I would be alright in his absence and sent him on his way back to the village. But forlornness descended as I watched him through the nail holes, making his way back down the mountain. Leaving me to my lonely silence.

14

I don't want to bore you with too much of that circumcision stuff and all that comes with it. But I must tell you about the hardship of that first day and, in particular, the agony that comes with the night. The pain is hard to describe. It is a shocking pain that hits you like electrocution. In such extreme suffering, it is important to remind yourself that your time there is not only about getting through the pain. The lack of food, sleep, water, the burning agony, are something to be endured not just physically, but metaphorically. As a man, you don't give up, you don't break down. You do what you're supposed to do to see it through, without the dependency on others. You hold on with tenacity until the process is complete. That's the important lesson.

'*Mkhwetha*, can I enter?' said the voice of my brother from outside.

I cannot put into words the relief, the liveliness and sense of security that filled the hut when my brother arrived. He had brought one of the dogs with him, as instructed. He chained it at the foot of the hut and leaned his shovel against the ribs of the hut. Then on his own initiative he began to make fire. Warmth and comfort rose out of the smoke. He brought me some fresh maize, too; it was softer this time. Above all, he had brought me himself. He was going to spend the night with me. The chest people felt like all they needed was there right now.

'So, did you manage to ask whether anyone else had phoned, like?' I took the dangerous route and asked the pressing question. It was dangerous because I already knew the answer. And hearing it was going to hurt.

'Yes, I asked. They said Mother had phoned again to check if I had been to see you. That's all, *mkhwetha*,' he said matter-of-factly.

'So, that's all?' I verified. I was hoping he had forgotten to add:

'And they say someone by the name of Yanga or Yanda had phoned asking for *mkhwetha*, but she did not leave a message.' But, no, my brother nodded his head to confirm that was all and no one else had phoned.

In hindsight, I think I totally downplayed my mother's caring concern because the person I was wishing would phone had not done so. In the light of Yanda's silence, it sounded to me like my brother was telling me that no one had phoned at all.

I inhaled a lungful of air and exhaled it slowly, hoping to release my disappointment along with it. The headrush and dizziness that resulted from the long exhalation managed to distract me a little.

I began to chew the grains while they were still warm. First, I emptied the enamel bowl that was still filled with the old grains. These were now rock hard. You could catapult a goose down with them. Then I poured the fresh maize in. Its yellowness made my stomach groan. I took a handful and stuffed my mouth with it. Although this time the maize was softer, it was still raw. I found it tiring to chew the flavourless kernels, but I kept my jaw moving.

My brother took the axe and went outside to make sure we had enough firewood for the night. I took the opportunity to do a quick dressing change in his absence.

Let me tell you, you may get disoriented as the days go by. You may forget who had visited and who said what. You might not remember what day it is. But I promise you, you will know what time of day it is. Your limb will tell you.

Mine did not disappoint. It informed me that the time was after 7pm. That's the time of the coming out of wild rabbits. You see, wild rabbits sleep by day and they come out just between sundown and dusk; it's a safety measure for survival purposes.

As I tried to bandage my limb with the leather thong, it told me in particular ways that it was the time of the rabbits. Those were the agonising ways that had me inventing new tactics to distract myself from the pain. I knelt down and began to move around on all fours, round and round inside the hut, like a dog that wants to sleep or a hen that wants to lay an egg. Yes, like that.

It was impossible to simply sit and do nothing. I needed the distraction of movement to take attention away from the agony between my legs. I crawled around like a *sangoma* who is trying to source wisdom from the dead, albeit without success. None of the excruciating sensation left my body. How to put into words that relentless agony? It felt like the chopping of the axe outside was hammering the pain into my limb. When the chopping stopped, I moved as swiftly as possible to regain my former position and make believe I was resting. I did not want my brother to see me in this bad shape. I buried myself under the white blanket, hiding the sweat that had begun to wipe off the thick clay from my face, and rocked my knees underneath the blanket.

The rest of the night was a repetition of this and worse. There was twisting and turning, kneeling and bending, clenching and unclenching of teeth, groaning and moaning, but all done under my breath so my brother would not hear. There were bitter moments of cold paralleled with blistering hotness. The pain did not remain at a constant intensity but came in waves, at estimated five-minute intervals. The pain was a sign that the herbs were doing their work of controlling any infection. As soon as it began to ease, it meant it was time to renew the herbs.

I had defeated the desire to sleep, but with difficulty. The snippets of snoring that came from my brother; my yawning and longing to rest; the peacefulness of the night, all whispered to my head people that I should just lie down on the blanket and steal a five-minute nap.

'Just five,' Satan's voice said.

'But what if you fall asleep properly? What will happen to your circumcision? And aren't you afraid that witches might come for you?' the head people protested.

'C'mon, it's just five minutes. You won't fall asleep. You will just rest your body, for just five, man,' Satan urged.

The way he said it was so alluring. The way he said "just" was so inviting. It made sleeping sound blissful and heaven-like. Imagine Satan making things seem heaven-like. I must confess, if it hadn't been for the fact that my brother was a sleep-talker, Satan would have won me over, ultimately.

'No one else phoned, I told you already, *mkhwetha*,' my brother said in his sleep.

That, what he'd just said, shocked away all thoughts of sleep with its blissful promises. The hut rose back to wakefulness. The fire had died. The dog had, somehow, entered and slept below my brother at the doorway of the hut. It pricked up its ears now that my brother began the conversation in his sleep.

I stared at him, checking that he was really asleep while he said the things he said. His hand was inserted inside his pants. It looked like he had a comforting grip right there. He certainly looked asleep. I wondered if sleep-talking was a way for a person's head people to release their unexpressed utterances. Like, if you wanted to anoint someone with a curse, it *sommer* comes out when you are asleep:

'You stinking son of a she-dog.' Or if you have feelings for someone, you simply tell her: 'You know what, I love you, *dammit*.' Wouldn't it be wonderful to hear the suppressed voices and unfinished sentences of people, and know what they were really thinking? Or would it be too dangerous? 'You know what, Mister *flippen* President, you suck.'

My brother was still going on with his sleep mumbling: 'No, no one else phoned, *mkhwetha*. Yes, I'm sure... Who are you expecting to hear from anyway?... A girl...? We're not supposed to talk about snots here, *Oom* Dan told you... No. I won't leave you...'

I'm sure there was still more stuff coming but at that moment the dog remembered it was a dog and belonged outside. The noise of its chain grating against the zinc sheets interrupted my brother's conversation with himself.

Timely as ever, my limb let me know it was sunrise. As soon as day came, some of the painful stiffness left it, and it became easier to work with again. I shuddered to imagine another coming of dusk. I have to say, that was one of the hardships that MC-Squared hadn't properly explained to me. Perhaps he had been shielding me.

It was about now that I first noticed strange things happening in my manhood. Not in the circumcision, but in the head. The circumcision was looking fine – I mean as fine as you could expect under the circumstances. But the head worried me. There was this sogginess in it, around the glans penis. It began to drip down like melting ice cream. It wasn't just water that dripped from it, there was something red that diluted it. It looked like my flesh. Yes, it was my flesh. My body had begun to drip its own flesh away. There was a foul smell that came from the dripping. Unlike the circumcision, it wasn't painful. It just melted and dissolved, eating itself away like a cigarette smokes itself away.

I knew at that point that something had gone wrong. I just did not know it was going to be as bad as it turned out to be. I had no idea that this was the ultimate turning point of my life.

That my metamorphosis had begun.

I asked my brother to go and call Grandfather, failing to suppress the emotion behind my request. In the absence of any attendant, I badly needed someone here who could explain things to me. I needed to be told if I'd done something wrongly, and shown how to correct it.

Where was *Ta*'Yongs? Or MC-Squared, with all his wealth of knowledge? Where was *Oom* Dan with his pool of experience? I even found myself wishing that Uncle had returned from his sheep-shearing and would surprise me by walking in.

As the day wore on, the head of my limb began to waste away more hungrily, as if it was a fag being dragged on by an addictive smoker. Unlike the bulginess of earlier, there was now an alarming deflated look about it. The colour was an unhealthy grey and the smell of decay had worsened. Flies started to wander about, buzzing, as if sniffing the rot.

It was then that I began to wish for the nurses' visit. The thought that, if they didn't come, I might have to go to the hospital troubled me a great deal. At first, I resisted the idea, wrestling with it inside my skull. The voice of *Oom* Dan was clear in my head: what happens at the mountain stays at the mountain. To transgress this taboo was not a decision to be taken lightly. I was aware that to do so would have heavy consequences, would be to betray the culture and flout the customs of my people.

That heavy knowledge weighed on me all through the day, fighting with my growing concern about my limb. Watching the deterioration, it became ever clearer to me that if I was not to lose my limb – even, my life – I needed medical intervention, urgently.

15

It was already afternoon when my brother returned with another tin can full of maize. I'd been hoping he would return with Grandfather. But he came alone.

'*Mkhwetha*, can I enter?'

'Yes, come in,' I said.

The sacks at the entrance of the hut were pushed aside and a silver can made its way in, followed by the small body of my brother. The glare of light from the sky that blasted in with him was blinding to me. I had not seen light in two days now.

My brother crawled in and shot his questioning eyes at me. He wanted to know if I was still holding on. I gave him a well-rehearsed I-am-doing-fine look. But he did not seem convinced. I don't think my appearance was reassuring.

'Let's see what you have this time,' I said, avoiding asking him the obvious. It was clear from the fact that he'd come alone, and the worry on his face, that he was not bringing good news. He handed me the tin can. It felt heavier than usual. I must have lost some energy over these past two days and one whole night. That's how heavy it felt: two days and one whole night.

'What do you have in here, stones?' I joked. He grinned a little at my comment while he ruffled the dog gently between its ears. I opened the tin can. The yellow grains inside it were still warm. I could feel steam as I scooped up a handful. They were softer this time but my jaw was tired, as if I had a jawbone tremor.

'*Eish, mkhwetha...*' my brother said, and threw himself against the hut, causing the whole structure to tremble. He cupped his hand against his forehead, as if checking the temperature. Tears rolled down without warning from his eyes. It seemed that these tears had been withheld for a long while. Now they erupted. That's all there was, just the tears. No sobbing, moaning or hiccupping.

'You can't start crying now, *mfethu*,' I said, trying to encourage him to be strong.

He used the backs of his hands to mop the tears. But there were too many of them, and his hands were soon soaked. He pulled his T-shirt up and used that to wipe his eyes instead.

I swallowed and cleared my throat. My Adam's apple was sore and my voice box felt shrunken. I swallowed and swallowed, like a frog in suspension.

There was silence.

'So, did you find him?' I finally asked.

'Yes. But he was still in his bedroom, and Grandmother was there. So I had to wait till he got up,' he said. His T-shirt looked like it had been chewed and spat out by a calf. It was wrinkled and moist. He fiddled with it as he spoke. His fingernails had the usual greyness to them. He chewed the nails so thoroughly that the fingertips looked like wooden logs.

I swallowed again, conscious of my thirst. I had been thirsty since yesterday but had resolved to push it from my mind. Water is not allowed here. I'd urinated only once since I got here and it had been a struggle. The acidity of my urine had felt like an electric shock whamming my limb. I had also sweated a lot the previous night, and the temperature of the day hadn't been kind, either. The result was that I had lost a lot of water, and now my thirst was starting to torment me.

An idea suddenly hit me. I took up the tin can and drained

the tiny drops that had settled at the bottom due to the evaporation taking place inside. It was just sufficient to fill two teaspoons, but it lubricated my oesophagus enough to temporarily quench my thirst.

'I don't think Grandfather is coming,' my brother said.

'Why not?'

'Because, he said...' my brother faltered, then continued, 'he was angry, *mkhwetha*...'

Another pause, 'He said... "what kind of *ndoda* is this your brother going be when he is so fragile?" Like that, *mkhwetha*,' my brother said.

He went on: Grandfather had told him to *voetsek*. He said he must never come to him with such nonsense again. Didn't my brother know that what happens at the mountain stays at the mountain? Well from now on he must let it sink into his head: the business of the mountain has no place in the village. Grandfather then asked no one in particular: 'What business do I have with goats at my age, anyway?'

It was from this that my brother concluded that our grandfather was not going to respond to my request.

'Alright,' I said, though my voice did not sound very alright, 'we'll see.'

'Should I call *Oom* Dan, *mkhwetha*?' my brother asked.

I was pleased with his quick mind. What he was suggesting was not out of the question. The head people said that *Oom* Dan was someone I could rely on. But the problem was that you could not have another man intervening in the business of a man's kraal. *Oom* Dan could only offer help if it was asked for by Grandfather. Not because I called him, or merely out of his own will. So to get *Oom* Dan, I would have to go through Grandfather. It seemed impossible under the circumstances. Even to have had *Oom* Dan there during my going-in ceremony had been lucky chance.

'No,' I said, 'don't call him yet. Let's first see what your grandfather will do. If he doesn't come, then you can call *Oom* Dan.'

My brother looked at me like I was crazy. In hindsight, I know what was going through his head at that moment. I mean, you can't just stand by idly and not seek help when you fear your brother is dying. You query the sanity of anybody who suggests patience in such circumstances, especially if it is the person in question. In fact, you assume that such madness is symptomatic of his impending death. That was the way my brother looked at me then.

'Will you please help me with this,' I said, handing him the white clay I'd rubbed from the rocks while he was gone. I was inviting him to touch my body and feel that I was not dead yet.

'The whole body, *mkhwetha*?' he asked.

'Start with the face, *mfethu*.'

'You want to be a goat,' he joked.

I smiled at that. I liked the fact that his head people were being whisked away from complicated worries by the distraction of the task. Ten-year-old children don't deserve burdensome thoughts such as he was wrestling with. I liked the change of mood.

'You are already feeding me raw grains; you might as well whiten me to complete my being a goat,' I said, fuelling the small talk.

He began to smear my face, starting with the forehead. There was a tolerable coldness about the clay. He smeared some more, turning his head this way and that, as *Bra*'Mtyobo does when he does his artwork on the face of his house. He complained that I was distracting him with the movement of my temples while I munched on grains.

'Tell me, who is distracting who here?'

'You are, *mkhwetha*.'

'So, I am distracting you? Am I not busy eating? Are you not the one distracting me with your mud?' I said, happy to tease my brother.

I put the tin can down and held still for him to finish smearing me. He applied the clay round my eyes, down the nose, round the lips, cheeks and chin. The thick mask was already drying on my forehead. It felt like my face was heavily make-upped.

My brother descended to my neck, shoulders and arms. It was colder when he began to do my torso and back. He laughed when he got down to below my belly button; the hair around there must have been the source of his amusement. I know the mischievous thoughts that arrest you as a child when you see pubic hair on grown-ups. You start imagining what lies below, the shape of things, especially if it belongs to *mkhwetha*.

I closed my eyes and listened to my limb dripping away. I pictured the flesh dropping onto the white blanket, staining it red. It had been dripping this way since sunrise. *I will have no penis left by tomorrow if it continues to leak away at the rate that it does now*, I thought. The chest people shuddered in alarm at that prospect.

Again, I became aware of the rot smell, its offending whiffs. My attention was drawn to it by the green helicopter that landed on my nose. Earlier I'd made a little fire to create a smokiness that would both mask the odour and chase the flies away. It had worked for a while. But now that there was no smoke, the odour of my fetid state was back.

'We are done now; we'll do the bottom after...' I began, then paused, taken aback that I'd already forgotten how many days were left before my seclusion ended. I quickly counted the stones around the fireplace and said '... after six days, when I can walk around.'

I thought about asking whether Uncle had returned but it did not seem like a good topic to raise. It would only remind me of what I did not want to think about. There was one question that I could not avoid asking, though.

'You didn't forget to check if someone phoned asking for me, did you?'

'I did ask. They said there was no message for you,' my brother replied.

Dusk, the unavoidable, arrived once again. My time-conscious limb alerted me to it. As before, a severe sense of tenderness phased in, throwing the limb in question into pulsating agony. The strap seemed to shorten and the limb became stiff and difficult to work with. I could feel my heartbeat pounding in it.

The last of the day had passed without the hoped-for visit from Grandfather. I was now plotting my next move. Unfortunately, this subsequent step, unavoidable though it was, involved the unthinkable: a trip to the hospital. I had thought about my situation in between the hellish imaginary five-minute intervals of changing the dressing. I knew I had only two choices: either I defied the notion that what happens at the mountain stays at the mountain, and never became a man in the eyes of my community, or I lost my whole manhood and buried it at the mountain – and, perhaps, even my life itself. Either way, it was apparent that I had overstayed my welcome here.

The idea of turning up at the hospital sooner rather than later had been delayed by my hope that the nurses' visit might still happen. When they did not come the first day, I assumed that they were attending to the Sada initiates first, and would get round to me afterwards; we of the villages are always considered last on things. But two full days and one whole night had come and gone without any sign of them. I had to conclude that they weren't going to appear at all.

The other reason why I hadn't turned myself in at the hospital yet was that I still clung to the possibility that Uncle might return from his sheep-shearing and come to see how I was doing. But that hope, too, remained cheated.

The next step in my plan was to call for *Oom* Dan. This was the time to stop caring about protocol and focus on doing what had to be done. If that alternative also failed to materialise, then I would have to move onto the last resort, which was to take myself to hospital.

It was the best plan I could come up with under the

circumstances. I had no attendant to advise me, and in all the time that I had been on the mountain, no one had come to see how I was. The village men were obeying Grandfather's orders not to stray around my hut. If they had been allowed to participate in my grooming, as is normally the case, this thing would have been detected in its early stages and acted upon, somehow. Men always have some plan. For instance, there was I, not even a real man yet, but I had something planned.

I didn't know what Grandfather's motives were for marshalling the men away from me. If they were well-intended, because he cared about me and wanted to protect me from the kind of abuse that was sometimes dealt out to initiates at the mountain, then I dare say his love was proving fatal. And I won't act contrite for going against his orders.

The rot in my limb did not have the patience to wait things out. I saw its hungriness in the way it turned my flesh yellow and oozy. There was a general numbness in the head now. It felt - no, it did not feel - it was as if it was somebody else's limb, not exactly attached to me.

The drowsiness accumulated from two full days and one whole night of no sleep began to consume me. It made me see things in twos and from a distance, like a drunk man. I watched my limb drip away with vagueness. There were times I caught myself falling onto the fire, or against the zinc ribs of the hut.

'*Mkhwetha*, can I -?'

'Come in, *mfethu*,' I said. I was delighted to finally have my brother back again, for I was starting to feel totally abandoned.

'You are back late. What happened?'

'I went to collect sheep first.'

'Where was Grandfather?'

'He went to attend the coming in of *abakhwetha* at Sbenga's place.'

'Oh, so they finally arrived?'

'*Ja, mkhwetha.*'

'Alriiiiiight. So you went to gather the sheep?'

'*Ja, mkhwetha*. I wish I had known earlier that Grandfather wasn't going to collect them, because then I could have done so after hunting for these leaves,' he said.

'So you went to collect the herbs as well?'

'*Ja*. Here you go, *mkhwetha*.'

'But I can't use them, you took them to the village. You know *mos*, mountain things must stay at the mountain, remember?'

'I know. I collected them and hid them under a tree. Then I had to go back and collect them from that same spot when I had gotten the food and the dog from home. That is why I was so late today. I wish I had just brought them here at once but I wanted to make one trip, *mkhwetha*.'

As he spoke, he was busy chaining the dog at the foot of the hut. I had requested that he take it back with him that morning because we had noticed it wasn't eating the raw grain leftovers we fed it, and we were afraid it would starve. So, he had taken it with him, promising that when he came back he would make sure to bring food for both the dog and me.

'Just remember I'm not a dog, not any more, *kwedini*,' I joked, as I watched him finish the chaining.

'*Ja*, I'll tell them, you're a goat,' he grinned in reply.

Grandfather must have drowned himself at Sbenga's that day. That's what he does, he drowns himself in alcohol. My grandfather is the type of drinker that doctors will advise to continue drinking, because without it he would just die. He empties the bottle and then he walks, no, he frogmarches all the way home, as if he'd put his legs inside the bottle from which he'd emptied the alcohol. Today must have been one of those days where he seemed bottled.

It was news to me that Sbenga's grandsons had arrived. My brother told me they were located on the opposite side of the village, near Ox-Kraal bladder. I asked who their attendant was, plotting to send my brother over there to call him to come to me, whoever it was. He said he did not know. Well, that was understandable. It was not a matter for boys and women to know about, after all. It was one of those what-happens-at-the-mountain-stays-at-the-mountain things.

I hadn't even known that there were two other initiates being sent to the mountain that day. There'd been rumours as far back as November that Sbenga's grandsons were due to come from Cape Town, but they still hadn't turned up by the time I went off and I hadn't enquired further. Consumed as I was by the goings-on in my hut, I'd totally shut out the happenings in the rest of the world. I guess the head people had adopted a what-happens-at-the-village-stays-at-the-village attitude. It was safer that way.

Before my going to the mountain, my brother and I used to talk about many things, including, of course, women. Yes, he was already aware at that age, so there was nothing to hide. In fact, he sounded more knowledgeable than I was about such things. He shocked me when he told me he'd once consumed a bird already. Ten-year-olds having sex! The head people hoped it was just an empty boast, but the other part wanted to ask my ten-year-old brother what it was like the first time. There hadn't been a real first time for me yet, remember. Only a couple of imaginaries, though they'd all been blissful.

Anyway, such talk was to be avoided here. By talking of sex, my brother and I would be violating the law of the mountain. We, at least I, the initiate, wasn't supposed to even think about snots. Especially not the bliss confined between their thighs. Lest it made me... you know, and caused trouble with my circumcision.

Now that Sbenga's sons had finally arrived, I could imagine the critical way the villagers would be looking at them, sizing them up and inventing derogatory anecdotes about them. Local folklore had it that city boys struggled more than their village counterparts when it came to endurance at the mountain. There were many stories about city boys attempting to escape from the mountain, shedding tears during the aftercare, or secretly drafting letters to their mothers – which would later be confiscated and made public narratives – and other unmanly things like that. It was expected – no, it was hoped – that Sbenga's boys were going to treat us villagers to some spectacular unforgettables. Little did the village suspect that it was, in fact, one of its own sons who would turn out to provide the much-anticipated drama.

16

I heard someone call my name. It was the voice of a man, but high-pitched. I recognised the voice as Rain's. I had seen him in the distance going past my hut on his way to bring the cattle down for milking. He was easy to recognise because of his limp. I had watched him through the tiny nail-hole chinks, hoping he would decide to come and visit, the way that men do with initiates. But like all the men, he kept his distance, respecting the orders of Grandfather. Grandfather who, for his own reasons, had kept them all away but had not come even once to check how things were going with me.

I cannot express the relief I felt when I heard Rain's voice calling to me. He was calling my name from a distance, and I had to reply with baboon intonation. Every time he called my name I had to respond in the same way. It is the way initiates are expected to reply, like the baboons we are supposed to be. Whatever nonsense is called to you, you must answer in agreement in that particular way.

'I brought you sweets, *mkhwetha*?' Rain called out questioningly, as he approached with his uneven limping walk. His right leg was too short for its counterpart. It's the way he was born.

'*Boogroom*,' I roared in answer.

'Do initiates eat sweets?'

'*Boogroom*.'

'I brought you good news?'

'*Boogroom.*'
'I brought you healing?'
'*Boogroom.*'
'I brought you life?'
'*Boogroom.*'
'I can't hear?'
'*Boogroom.*'
'What is that?'
'*Boogroom.*'
'Is that a baboon?'
'*Boogroom.*'
'Sounds like a snot to me?'
'*Boogroom.*'
'I can't hear?'
'*Boogroom.*'
'Are you sleeping?'
'*Boogroom.*'

The head people ran about chaotically as I boomed back from inside the hut. I quickly scanned around me, trying to spot anything that might be construed as evidence of mischief going on here. But I couldn't see anything. I held my stick ready to use to shake hands with Rain. In the code language of the mountain, an initiate is an animal and therefore must avoid physical contact with people. The knobkerrie is also symbolic of the penis, and must be handled carefully by the man coming in. The way he shakes your hand through the knobkerrie shows whether he respects you or not.

I counted the stones around the fireplace; only five left. I was glad that my brother was away and not there to witness my vulnerability. By this time, I was not even able to sit up. I was also not sure how to handle myself in front of another man, since there had been no one to instruct me.

A visit from a village man is considered to be a dreadful thing by some initiates, for men have the power to do what they want to you, to punish you for small mistakes or avenge themselves for past behaviour, as the case may be. Also, you don't want another man's hand handling your limb in its painful state. But this was not the case for me. Yes, I was anxious, but I was also desperate for guidance. This visit of Rain's was going to put things into perspective about how I should deal with my decaying body.

The dog did not give Rain any problems. It recognised him, since he often visited our house. He was my mother's distant cousin and used to go hunting with my uncle. The dog knew him well from those excursions. He called it by its name.

I was ready for Rain. I had covered my body with the once white blanket, as custom demanded, and had my stick in my hand, ready for the handshake. Rain pulled back the maize-sack door. He pulled it so roughly that I began to shiver.

'You farted in here, *mkhwetha*. Didn't you?' were his first words.

'Uh-mm...' I said, not knowing whether to admit guilt or deny it.

'Come outside. I can't be suffocated by an initiate's fart. Come.'

'But...'

'I said come outside. It is me who says so. This one day you spent here has hardened your testicles. You have the nerve to backchat me. You think you are a man now. We will see about that. Come out.'

I collected a handful of herbs and my stick, wrapped myself with the blanket and crawled outside. Not very long ago my brother had smeared my face with white clay again. I was ready to meet visitors. I struggled with the light. It shot between my eyes and made me dizzy. I don't know what happened in the next few seconds.

When I regained consciousness, I was already seated against the ribs of my hut, outside.

The mountain side was green and healthy around me. There were patches of brown earth intermingled with green grass. The cows grazing in the distance looked gigantic and bestial. I heard the familiar buzz of sounds drifting up from the village, an indistinguishable cacophony of birds, chickens, animals and people. The air tasted fresh and moist after the confines of the hut. I struggled to inhale, for the freshness stung my nasal canals.

'I suppose this is your first time outside.'

'Yes... *Ta* Rain... my first time.'

'I saw that by the way you fell down. But where is your attendant?'

'I don't have one.'

'What do you mean? Where is your uncle?'

'He went sheep-shearing the day I came in.'

'So he has never been here?'

'Never.'

'What does your old man say about organising you one?'

'That one!' I said, and did not regret having referred to my Grandfather with such contempt. 'He has never been here either. I sent for him and he told my brother that he, my grandfather, has no business here and that I must stop being so fragile.'

'Did you have a fall out with him before coming here?'

'No.'

'So how have you been keeping up with the work then?'

'Have a look for yourself.'

'You are a brave initiate. You are handing yourself over to another man's hand, just like that. Brave initiate. Brave.'

There was silence.

'Right,' he said, 'let us see.'

'Should we not go inside, like?' I asked.

'No need. Let us do it here. Don't be scared. I am a man, too, am I not?'

I peeled open the blanket for the first time outside. And there it was. Erect and tightened with a thong; my limb. The head, which is what Rain must have noticed first, had turned like raw fat, yellow and revolting. There was a not-fit-for-human-consumption look about it.

'Have you been cooking this penis or what?' Rain asked, accusingly.

'It just turned like this one morning and...'

I said "one morning" like it was something that happened last December. But the way he asked that question, *maan*, had I been cooking my penis? Is that how it looked, cooked?

'I will find the reason you are so ripened. It is here, inside the hut. I will bring it to you; you wait here,' Rain said matter-of-factly. Then he went inside. There was the noise of tin cans banging against zinc walls, of sacks being ripped. It sounded like he dug some stuff up as well. The head people were rushing about, trying to verify if there was any incriminating evidence I might have left lying about. When I was a child, it was the same; if Grandmother said someone among us kids was stealing her sugar from the bin, I got palpitations, even though I wasn't guilty. Then I would usually end up admitting guilt, because I was identified as the one with the guiltiest appearance. This time, too, even though I knew I had been doing things according to the rules, I still had palpitations as if I had done something wrong.

'What else have you been eating other than the maize?' *Ta* Rain asked.

The way he said that, it was like my guilt was assured, like he already knew I was consuming something illegal that he could not put a name to just yet, and was thus asking me, the sinner, to name.

The discoloured whites of his eyes protruded as if they were about to pop out.

'Nothing, there is nothing else I ate.'

'How much water have you consumed?'

'None.' I swallowed, as a mental picture of two teaspoons appeared on the screen in my head.

Rain went on with his questions. Had I slept with a woman

during the night vigil? Was I smoking anything? Had I been sleeping when I was not supposed to? Was I sure I had not drunk any water? Then he began to suggest that there must have been bewitchment of some sort. Who was the grandmother of my girlfriend? This question was painful. It made me picture Yanda's *gogo* standing on the red *stoep* with Days beside her. Nothing potentially evil about that. Nonetheless I told Rain I did not have a girlfriend, though I was somewhat embarrassed to admit this. He then asked something I'd ruled out completely as a possible factor: my real clan name. He knew that my mother's clan name was Yirha, so what he was asking was my father's. I told him I was a Dlamini, of the lineage of Jama, Sjadu, Gabhel'ekomini and so on. He then asked if the people of my father had been present at my coming-in ceremony. What he was really wanting to know was according to whose clan my ritual was conducted, Dlamini or Yirha? Since there wasn't any involvement from my father's side, I told him it was my mother's. He gave me a look that proclaimed 'Strange!' I knew that by asking these questions, he was trying to exclude a possible fault in the cultural practice that would have suggested my father's ancestors were angry with me, and that this was their way of admonishing me. I responded with a sneer that I hoped conveyed what I thought of that suggestion. Finally, Rain came to what I considered to be my real problem: the limb in question.

'Can I see how you do this thing first, before I give you my own hand,' he said. That giving of his hand thing sounded scary to me. It would be my first time to get a hand from someone else, after Geca, of course. And if Geca's hand was anything to go by, then I was in for some gruelling stuff, I thought.

I undid the thong. Rain had a look at my limb.

'I can say that the main thing you are here for, there is no problem around that, *mkhwetha,* you are basically...' he started to say, and then decided against it in mid-sentence, the way men do. He never did complete that sentence. But it wasn't hard to conclude that he had wanted to say I was basically almost a man. Almost. How pleased I was to learn this.

He watched me while I wrapped and tightened the thong, and he did not look too disappointed with my skills there either, though he did not comment on them. I took it that he was satisfied with my hand. If I was doing so well in terms of my circumcision, then why had the head of my limb gone rotten? he wondered aloud. He confessed that he'd never seen anything like it. Nor could he think of any useful suggestion to curb the problem. And then he asked me something I wasn't expecting.

'What are you going to do with this?'

There was silence as I digested his question. It surprised me that he should be asking me to name the solution.

'I don't know...' I said. But it was the kind of "I don't know" that suggested I had more to say.

'But what do you have in mind?' he prompted.

I told him that I had called for Grandfather, and he had replied in the way I had described. Uncle, my attendant, had chosen to go sheep-shearing, as I had already told him. So what I was thinking was that I wanted to call *Oom* Dan. I wanted to do this so he could be the one to endorse my decision; my decision being to seek medical help. I was surprised that *Ta* Rain didn't seem surprised when I mentioned this. But I was disappointed by his reaction, too. I mean, you would rather have someone shout that they disagree with your announcement, than be met with the mute approach adopted by so many village men. Rain just listened as if not too interested in what I had to say. I told him that as he could see, none of this was of my making. The fact that I was still there and had done so well meant that I did want to see things through, but fate had decided that I had overstayed my welcome.

'Have you sent for Dan already?'

'Not yet. I was intending to do that towards the end of

the day. I'm hoping...' I started to say, then decided against confiding the hope I had for the nurses' visit. I assumed Rain wasn't aware of the recent decision by the Department of Health, and I didn't feel like having to start unpacking the whole policy for him. So I just shut up at that point.

'Whatever you are going to do, you need to do it fast, *mkhwetha*. There's no point in you staying on, only to lose that very thing you're meant to build here. I am not giving you licence to act inappropriately, but you have to act quickly. That's what I'm going to say to you. Act quickly, or lose it all, *mkhwetha*,' he said.

Apart from validating my plan, Rain also reactivated my anxiety. It hit me forcefully from his words that the situation was urgent and out of hand. It wasn't enough that I was holding onto hope, still trying to be the man I was expected to be. I needed to act, as he said.

When I looked at my limb again after Rain had left, I saw its weariness. I saw the reason for Rain's bewilderment. It was rapidly falling apart. I now had to remove tissue wreckage from the thong every five minutes. Rain had brought home to me that I was subjecting myself to more harm by continuing to stay there. He'd pointed out the signs of dehydration and had even given me permission to have a cupful of water every day.

'One cupful, no more,' he emphasised, stressing that it was important that there were fluids in my body for it to function properly. Here I was with my university-entry-level intelligence, being taught simple biology by an illiterate villager. Where was my brain all this time?

I grew angry with myself and the world in general. Why was I being subjected to so much suffering? What had I done to deserve this? True, I had made mistakes in my life and my past had been far from exemplary. But in the matter of my circumcision, I was doing everything required from me. I surely didn't deserve to have it all fall apart this way.

I resolved that the moment my brother came back, I would

send him to call *Oom* Dan. There was no longer any doubt
that he needed to be brought into the picture right away. I
had Rain's encouragement to act, but I needed *Oom* Dan to
legitimise my dishonourable plan. I did not want it to sound
like I had been defeated. It was manhood in general that had
been defeated. And manhood was a phenomenon of which
Dan was an embodiment.

It was far preferable that he should take me to hospital than
that I should escape there by myself. If he was the one to
escort me, people were more likely to give me the benefit of
the doubt. The story would sound like it should: I had put up
a good fight at the mountain; I did not fail or simply succumb
because I wasn't up to the hardship. I wanted everyone rather
to be saying of me: 'If it wasn't for *Oom* Dan, he would be
dead.'

Besides which, Dan was the one best placed to intervene
since he knew the onset of the story. He had been there at
my going-in ceremony and had witnessed my grandfather's
shameful absence with his own eyes. At this point, his relations
with his *sbali* were the least of my worries.

17

Sbenga's son pulled up at the emergency entrance of Dongwe hospital and killed the engine of the brown Toyota Hilux van. There was a moment of ringing silence, overriding the moan of the cooling engine. I felt the eyes of Grandfather and Sbenga's son staring at me from both sides. I was sitting between them, wrapped in my stained white blanket, pressed between Grandfather's thigh and the gear lever.

'I will wait with the car, *bawo*,' said Sbenga's son to Grandfather. It was the only thing he'd said since we'd left the village. All the way here he had been listening to Grandfather's monologue, nodding and humming his agreement to everything. The first thing Grandfather had said when we got into the car was: 'I don't know what has gotten into the youth of today. You are so fragile. Mmh?' He made it sound like he was incorporating all the youth of South Africa in that statement, including Sbenga's son. I think it was Grandfather's way of gagging him from making any unwelcome comments. His job was simply to deliver us to our destination, as he had been instructed to do by his old man.

Now he sat hugging the steering wheel, waiting hopefully to be told that no, he should come into the hospital with us. But all Grandfather said was: 'Mmh... thank you Sbenga's son. I doubt we will be very long here.'

He opened the door and manoeuvred himself out the van. The heat of his thigh left a numb imprint on my own thigh.

I couldn't remember when last my body had rubbed against another's. It had felt unpleasant to sit squashed up so closely against my enemy on the front seat of the van. But there was nothing to be done except put up with it. By that stage, I wanted so badly to be going where we were heading that I would have endured any discomfort.

I smuggled myself out of the car, careful not to expose my white-smeared body or, worse, my... you know what.

'Leave that thing behind!' ordered Grandfather, indicating my knobkerrie. There was anguish in his voice. I put the knobkerrie back in the van and closed the door behind me. Sbenga's son got out and stood next to his father's Hilux, his hands in his pockets like the spectator he was on this night. I envied him his freedom.

Following Grandfather into the hospital, I found it difficult to walk upright. My back ached and my joints were jellylike. This was not surprising, since I'd spent the last three days sitting down or crawling around without ever fully straightening my body. It was hardly more than a few metres from the van to the hospital entrance but already I was needing a long rest to catch my breath. The head people pointed out that it was the last thing I could request from Grandfather at this moment. I tailed after him at my snail's pace, wishing that *Oom* Dan was with us, or that it had been him alone who'd brought me here. He had offered to come, but Grandfather had assured him he didn't need his help. The head people of Grandfather were probably whispering that *Oom* Dan had done enough damage already. After all, this was Grandfather's kraal he was trampling upon, so he'd better tread carefully. I think *Oom* Dan got the message loud and clear.

I'd sent for *Oom* Dan that evening as soon as my brother came back to the hut. The limb had let me know it was evening in the usual way, by becoming painfully difficult to work with. The head people responded: we are not spending another dusk here, they insisted.

I heard the footsteps of my brother outside, and the dog moaning at the sight of him bringing its portion of food. He came crawling in, and as always, the sight of him reassured me. When I relayed my instructions to him, he reacted with glad relief. I didn't even need to tell him what to say to *Oom* Dan, only that I thought it was time he was called to come to the mountain.

'Okay, *mkhwetha*,' he said with immense pleasure.

He put the tin can down and crawled out of the hut.

Night had fallen by the time *Oom* Dan arrived. He had come alone. When he looked at me, I could see the shock of my dilapidation written on his face. His molars ground themselves together and his temples pulsed violently. His dark face, hugged by its white beard, was as sombre in the lamplight as if he'd come to announce the sudden death of so and so.

'The times are changing, grandson,' *Oom* Dan said.

That's what he said: the times are changing. Then he added: 'And it seems we have no choice but to adapt to them.'

I presumed that he was referring to the way the circumcision process was carried out these days. I waited for elaboration, but it never came. Grown-ups were like that; they liked frustrating us with parables.

I told Dan why I'd sent for him. Like Rain, he listened passively, without so much as a nod to indicate his thoughts on what he was hearing. His silence made me anxious because I had no idea whether he thought I was talking rubbish or understood my situation. Still without a word he gazed unblinkingly at the limb as I showed it to him in illustration of my decomposing genitalia.

Only when I'd finished and covered myself up again did he finally respond. He sighed a long sigh of dismay, and then he spoke.

Let me tell you, when there is something really wrong with you, you know there is something wrong but you don't want to admit to yourself just how bad it is. You constantly read from

what others say about your situation in order to discern the
extent of your trouble. It is from their reactions that you gain
hope or lose it. And so, even though I had already told *Oom*
Dan what I thought should be done next, I was still hoping he
would burst into laughter and tell me how foolish I was even
to suggest such a thing. That my situation could be handled
easily at the mountain, without the need for hospital; and that,
actually, it was something quite normal. I would have been
overjoyed to hear him say these things, for I would have known
then that it was only a matter of time before I became a man
in the expected way. And that, in fact, I might even create a
world record for fast healing. This victorious anecdote would
then be the story I would narrate to my own boys when they
underwent the same process in approximately the year 2042.

But that hope was lost the minute *Oom* Dan sighed his long
sigh of grief. And when at last he spoke, his words held no
comfort for me: 'Grandson, you have waited for too long,' he
said. Those were his exact words.

It felt as though I'd just been diagnosed with cancer of
the blood. Who else but *Oom* Dan was more qualified to
announce what he just had? Had he not been chosen by
me subconsciously for the very reason that he was a death
announcer? Now here he was, telling me that I was nearing
my grave. His words made me feel as though I was being
circumcised all over again, only this time in an important
organ inside my chest. My left lung. No. My heart. It was my
heart that was being subjected to circumcision by *Oom* Dan's
heavy words. Words can circumcise, did you know that? I
realised it at that moment.

It was the barking of the dog that roused me from drowning
in the deep waters of my own despair. *Oom* Dan was talking
again. He was telling me that when my brother told him about
my request, he'd asked the boy if Grandfather, *Oom* Dan's
sbali, was already at the mountain. The boy had responded
'No'. *Oom* Dan had been puzzled by that response. How

could the initiate have sent for him before his own father?
he'd wondered. And then he'd asked the boy whether he'd
also been sent by the initiate to go and call his *sbali*. But the
boy had again responded 'No'. He'd read from the boy's
uninitiated face that something was seriously the matter.

'I was going to come straight away. Then I thought, no, let
me first send the boy to call *Sbali*, for reasons of respect for
another man's kraal. I told him to inform *Sbali* that it was I
and not the initiate that was calling him to the mountain. I
sensed difficulty, remembering that *Sbali* hadn't made it to
the mountain on the day of your coming in. *Nc, nc, nc...*' He
clicked his tongue in disapproval.

He went on about the haste with which he'd then hurried
to the mountain after receiving my brother's message, and
his difficulty in walking in the darkness of the mountain. He
wasn't even sure if he still remembered where the hut was
placed. It had been several days, after all, since he'd been
to the hut. Great was his relief when he glimpsed brightness
protruding from the nail holes in the zinc sheets. At first, he'd
mistaken it for the brightness of a baboon's eyes. But then the
barking of the dog reassured him that it was, indeed, the hut
that he'd helped to build.

As he spoke, the barking of the dog intensified. I knew that
it was Grandfather arriving. How swiftly he'd responded when
he was being called by another man!

'That must be *Sbali*,' *Oom* Dan said.

'*Voetsek*! *Voetsek*!' the voice of my grandfather cursed at the
poor dog.

Instead of feeling anxious and apprehensive as Grandfather
approached, I was gripped by a wave of anger. I searched
unconsciously for my knobkerrie. When I found it, I gripped
it in my hands and gazed at the narrow mouth of the hut.

'No, *mfowam*,' *Oom* Dan said. 'Things are not solved that
way between men. *Sbali* and I will lock heads. I have seen the
delicacy of the situation. Just wait for the verdict of the elders.

You have done the right thing, calling us when things turned ugly, although I still think you have waited too long. I suppose your bravery is commendable, but some things are dangerous, *mfowam*. As a man, you calculate your risks, remember that. Even so, leave the matter to us now. Exercise patience like a man. We are still your fathers!'

Oom Dan met Grandfather outside. Their baritones vibrated in the night. I could not quite pick up what they were saying to each other. After a lengthy time of conspiring between themselves, they both came inside, unannounced. I saw Grandfather for the first time in four days. The bags below his eyes had swollen, as they normally did when he'd been drinking a lot. It must have been the effects of all the brandy he had soaked in during the going-in of Sbenga's grandsons.

He was wearing his blue overcoat and those rough boots that had a steel nose. In his hand he held a knobkerrie. It was his walking knobkerrie, but today it looked more like a very long thin penis.

'*Kwedini*, let me see this penis of yours... I don't understand how fragile you children of today are... it's difficult just to nurse your own manhood back to health! What is it they teach you in these schools... *rha*!'

'Don't fight, *Sbali*, don't fight.'

Had it not been for the encouraging nods of *Oom* Dan, I doubt very much that I would have shown Grandfather my circumcision. It seemed disgraceful to me that he should only be seeing it at this stage. But you can't deny your own father the chance to see.

I took the handmade lamp and put it between my legs. And then I began to undo the thong, careful not to peel off too much rubble from the dripping head. Grandfather motioned with his finger that I should show him the circumcision, and I did. I looked into his eyes as I showed him this important part. Again, I felt anger at the knowledge that this was the first time he'd taken a look at it. He'd almost missed seeing

it at all. If I'd waited another day, he would not even have
known what the surgeon had done to me. For a moment he
stopped breathing. His glassy brown eyes seemed hypnotised
by the nearly healed look of my circumcision. Then his
face collapsed. He was disappointed. My grandfather was
disappointed that the cause of my problem was not what he
had thought – I would even go so far as to say he wished – it
was. Contrary to his preconceived notion of my "fragileness",
I was, indeed, a man. The circumcision had healed perfectly,
except for the rotting situation in the head of my penis.

His ultimate exhalation almost killed the burning of the
lamp. It was so huge a sigh you could imagine that his dark soul
was being persecuted by the brightness of the light. I began to
redo the thong. Without saying a word to each other or to
me, my visitors crawled out of the hut again: Grandfather first
and then *Oom* Dan. I heard their conversation in the darkness
outside.

'I hear you, *Sbali*... it is mouldy.' That was Grandfather's
voice.

'I am glad we see eye to eye *Sbali*... now we must act... the
sun has long set...'

Their voices were swallowed by the massive silence of the
mountain, as they walked further and further away from the
hut. Once again, as had so often been the case since I'd come
to the mountain, I was left staring at the head people for
answers that were not forthcoming.

Finally, I heard the baritone voices rumbling back towards
me from the distance. The dog began its groaning and I
warned it to be quiet.

I felt my anxiety rise again, realising that this was it; there
was nothing for it now except to see the last step of my plan
put into action. The elders didn't allow me too much time to
brood on this.

'I tell you Sbali, children are such a responsibility,' one of
them said.

Now what? I thought.

'*Kwedini,* come out already. We don't have all day,' said Grandfather.

And that was how I was told that my time at the mountain was finished. I took my knobkerrie and wrapped myself in the blanket. My clay make-up was still stubbornly on my face. Just before I killed the lamp, I noticed that there were still five stones left around the fireplace. I prayed silently that I would get treated quickly at the hospital, overnight, and be back here again before dawn. Otherwise those five remaining stones would be a constant reminder that I fell short of being a man. I unchained the dog and put stones on the sacks that covered the mouth of the hut to weigh them down. My soul mourned the abandoning of my hut.

When I looked up, I noticed there was a third person walking with us in the darkness. I made him out to be Sbenga's son. We walked in slow procession, with me bringing up the rear, the only person without shoes. It was *Oom* Dan who lagged behind to walk by my side, while Grandfather and Sbenga's son led the way, talking about the petrol expenses that the mother of this initiate was going to have to pay.

Sbenga's old Toyota Hilux stood waiting for us at the bottom of the mountain. Sbenga's son opened the passenger door and then went around to the driver's side. He turned the ignition a few times before the engine caught. There was a shattering brightness as the headlights came on. I knew I was supposed to get into the car but I waited for instruction. Even though it had been I who suggested the move to hospital, I pretended that I was now thinking twice about it. I wanted that little moment of hesitation to convey to my companions that it was not my first choice to go to that forbidden place, that I was being forced by the circumstances.

It was at that point that *Oom* Dan offered to come with us but he was dissuaded by Grandfather, politely. Grandfather ordered with a motion of his hand that I should get into the car first. He squeezed in next to me, banging the car door

several times before it shut properly. Sbenga's son put the
car in gear and we rattled away along the gravel road towards
Whittlesea and then Dongwe, where the hospital was.

The ride was very uncomfortable, for the route was
winding and bumpy. But that was not the only source of my
discomfort. There was a palpably angry Grandfather sitting
next to me. He was breathing like a *Durban July* horse after
the race. On my other side I could feel the eyes of Sbenga's
son, equally accusing. I kept my own eyes forward, staring into
the dark distance ahead. Curious moths bumped against the
windscreen, attracted by our headlights. They were not used
to such brightness at night. With my peripheral vision, I saw
the giant darkness of the two boobs on my far right and the
shining waters of Ox-Kraal bladder on my left. I imagined
the boobs suddenly collapsing onto the dam to produce the
biggest wave ever recorded. We wouldn't even have a chance
to see that wave, because we would be squashed by the
gigantic stone of the mountain. Then we would die en masse
and there would be no circumcision, or failure of it, to rectify.
And what a relief that would be.

18

It was morning in the ward. I woke to unfamiliar brightness. The blinds on the windows had been drawn open, though the windows themselves remained closed. I was to learn that they were left that way permanently, for reasons of hygiene. The lights were off and the brightness was all from the natural light outside. Our ward must have been on the west side, for the early sunlight did not shine directly into it. I felt homesick for my east-facing hut that looked out onto the dawn. I missed my view of cloudless sky through the holes in the sheets of zinc, with the light growing amber as the sun rose from behind the mountain. This view looked wrong to me. It was populated by the same thorn trees and aloe plants that I was used to, but the mountain seemed ugly and misshapen without the familiar boobs. It looked unfinished.

A short, full rounded nurse came into our ward and stood there looking at us. The arms of her spectacles appeared to be loose, for she must have pushed them back into position at least three times before she uttered a word. She greeted us in a scornful voice and we responded with reluctance – we being the two patients opposite me and myself. Little did we know that by our lukewarm response we were fuelling an already lit brazier. The short nurse broke into a mocking song:

Somagwaza, amagwala abalekile
Hay yoh weh

Iyho-hoho
Hay yoh weh
Somagwaza, ngizoy'gwaza le kwekwe.

She sang another version of *Somagwaza* sung during the different phases of the circumcision ceremony. The verse she chose was significant on this occasion, for it is the one that reports to the mythical Somagwaza that the cowards among them have chickened out. She was insulting us to our face for having landed up at the hospital – we cowards! She was bringing home to us the disgrace of our being survived by our empty huts at the mountain, impressing on us our invalidity, the manhood rejects that we had become by fleeing to the hospital and the sub-human status that we were about to assume in society as a result. Her reaction might seem extreme, but it was typical of the mockery and censure that we could expect to encounter outside.

I took an immediate dislike to this nurse. I rested my head back on the pillow, envying the two initiates next to me who never answered her or even retrieved their heads from under the white sheets. They were the two patients who occupied the beds on my left-hand side. I hadn't seen their faces since I had arrived at the ward, so I could only presume they were initiates – I mean failed men – because their faces, like mine, still bore traces of white clay.

When my eyes landed on them, I felt a jolt of anxiety sliding down my throat. I hadn't known whether to greet them or not. By greeting them I would be acknowledging our common shame and opening the way to awkwardness. What would we talk about? And what language would we use? As initiates, we were meant to speak in the code language of the mountain. To open your mouth wrongly was to subject yourself to scrutiny and give yourself away. Far better to remain silent and anonymous in such circumstances.

Ignoring the rest of us the nurse shuffled herself over to the beds of the two covered-up initiates. She had a wheezing breath, as if she was asthmatic. Her belly had two protruding slopes, one above and another below her bellybutton. It meant she could not bend forward easily.

'*Mkhwetha*!' she called out and then again in quick succession: '*Mkhwetha*!'

The way she hailed the two initiates was as if she was approaching their hut. It was the way men call out when they approach an initiate's hut, the way Rain had done with me. But she did it with such scorn in her voice that I felt my face twist into a grimace. The two initiates did not move. They lay with the white hospital sheets pulled over their heads and their knees drawn up, as they had done from the beginning. It was clear they were not asleep, but simply had no courage to face their world.

The nurse was about to do the inevitable. She positioned herself between the two beds, gripped both top sheets with her thick hands and yanked them away, leaving the bodies of the initiates exposed. Apart from the brutality with which she had performed the action, we were all embarrassed by the strong rot smell that assaulted the atmosphere from under those sheets. I had never imagined such a smell coming from a living human being. If I had thought my smell was foul, it was nothing compared to this.

I could not see the initiate in the far bed, but the one nearest me neither moved nor spoke. He kept his hands in the position they had been in before he was revealed, palms set flat to cover his face and the tips of his thumbs touching his earlobes. His body was covered, like mine, in a blue gown and I noticed there were rings of brown stains around the genital area.

The nurse was still berating us as she leaned over the two initiates to check their breathing.

'So you think you are men now, mmh? Well the men I know were made at the mountain, not in the comfort of white sheets!' she lashed out in her knowledgeable way, pulling the sheets back up again. No one answered her, at least not aloud.

She bent over with difficulty, checking something under the beds and I heard an object fall down, which I presumed to be her loose spectacles. She picked them up and jammed them back on her nose, then straightened up and walked round to my bedside. I readied myself not to answer anything this rude and unprofessional nurse might throw at me. But she didn't say anything.

She stood by the trolley table at the foot of my bed, perusing the grey folder that sat there. I saw her skew name tag and the head people quickly photographed what was written there: Mrs E. Yaziyo, Auxiliary Nurse. The name suited her, for *yaziyo*, loosely translated, means "Know-It-All". Adjusting her spectacles for the umpteenth time, Nurse Yaziyo dipped her forefinger in her saliva and flipped through the folder pages furiously, as if looking for something hidden between them. Then she stopped and ran her finger down the last page as if following the words one by one, her forehead furrowed and her eyes blinking frequently. Finally, she slammed the folder shut. I swallowed and waited for my fate to be spelt out for everyone in the ward to hear.

'So, this one has no catheter, just a drip,' she declared to herself. Wheezing, she walked away, knocking her spectacles back into position a final time as she left the ward. If ever I wished for a tsunami, for my giant wave from the Ox-Kraal dam to come crashing down and swallow us all, it was at that moment.

What havoc Nurse Know-It-All had created with her contempt! I felt violated and truly sub-human, and I'm sure I wasn't the only one. Again, I was conscious of that stinging pain near my ribcage, as if it was the chest people that had been circumcised. I missed my caring night nurse. She was not judgemental like Nurse Yaziyo. She'd seemed to understand not only my physical condition but the weeping of my soul as well.

Nurse Know-It-All returned to the ward. I heard the shuffling of her navy pushes in the corridor, and the noise of metal cans bumping against each other. These turned out to be the two big jugs she was carrying. She put one down beside each of my neighbours, who had once again burrowed beneath their white sheets.

Nurse Yaziyo vanished between their beds. It was quiet for a moment, except for the sound of her wheezing. Then we heard water drilling into one of the metal jugs. A warm, strong smell of urine suffused the air. Then, I saw the two initiates opposite me pulling their covers over their heads. So, I did the same.

The drilling of urine into the jugs went on for a while. When it had stopped, Nurse Yaziyo shuffled out of the ward again, accompanied by the slopping sounds of chock-full jugs.

I became aware of my own full bladder and wondered how I was meant to go to the toilet with that drip bag attached to my arm. I hated the fact that I would have to drag the whole damn contraption along with me. At least I didn't have to urinate through a pipe, like my neighbours did. I wondered if my situation would ever get to that stage.

Nurse Know-It-All came back for a third time, wheeling in small trolleys on which there were grey basins. She wheeled one over to each of us, draping our bed curtains closed behind her.

'Let us wash, *madoda*,' she instructed.

I was surprised by her use of the word, for it seemed uncharacteristic of her that she would refer to us as "men", considering how rude she had been not too long ago. I slid out of bed, careful not to mess up the drip thing, and felt the water in the basin with my fingers. It was lukewarm. This was a sensation I no longer identified with. When last had I had a bath?

Nurse Know-It-All opened my curtains and threw a white towel on my bed while I was still considering my next move. There was this feeling of violation that I felt every time she did something. It was the way she did things, so rough and insensitive, that got to me.

I took my gown off and was left naked. And there it was, that disturbing white bandage wrapped around the limb. I observed a brief moment of silence for myself, for my lost manhood. Then I took up the small bar of soap from the trolley and smeared my face and armpits with it. I rinsed my face in the basin and used the white towel to wipe it. It came up stained with brownness. With so much accumulated dirt to get rid of, I was forced to moisten the clean end of the towel and use it as a washcloth.

I had just finished wiping myself dry when Nurse Know-It-All came inside the curtain to strip my bed of its linen. She did not look at me or say anything. She simply pulled the linen from the bed with her usual violence, leaving the hospital mattress bare. I pulled my gown back on and peeped through the curtain. One of the two initiates from the opposite side was wheeling his trolley forward to park it next to the linen trolley at the mouth of the ward. I did the same. I had underestimated the soreness of my body and the stiffness which still gripped it. It seemed to take forever to pull my drip along and steer the basin trolley as far as the door. I felt the eyes of my fellow initiates boring into the back of my head, observing my weakness. And I hated it all. It made me feel like a patient, and I wasn't! I belonged in my hut on the mountain.

'Open your curtains if you are done, *madoda*,' Nurse Know-It-All instructed us.

Again, that word, *"madoda"*, instead of the rudeness I had come to expect from her. What kind of a changeable animal was this Nurse Know-It-All? Or had I perhaps misjudged her? Maybe I had needed to draw her scorn because I believed I deserved contempt. I was so wounded inside; I wanted to be mistreated by everyone, like the failed man I thought I was.

The two initiates in the opposite row and I opened our

curtains as ordered. We still hadn't said a single word to each
other.

I stole a glance at their faces and judged them both to be
younger than me. I noticed that the one on the far right
had squint eyes. The head people registered him as Shorty,
because he was the shorter in height. The other they christened
Tall, for obvious reasons. Tall had a smiling kind of face that
looked like he was about to crack a joke all the time, yet he
remained as silent as the rest of us.

As far as the two *ma-jugs* were concerned, I never did get
to see their faces in all the time I was there. They remained
under the sheets with their heads covered and never came
up for air, not even to eat. When it came to medication time,
Nurse Know-It-All always draped their curtains around their
beds before she saw to them.

Dressing change took longer with the two *ma-jugs*, so Nurse
Know-It-All left them for last. She started with Shorty, then
Tall, and then came to me. That first day was a particular
ordeal, because I didn't know what to expect from the hand
of this nurse. She pulled my bed curtains closed and pushed
her short trolley inside, with its paraphernalia of scissors,
bandages, spatulas, gauze swabs, saline water, tapes and that
marmite thing. I hated handing myself over to her.

She removed my bandage and peeled the gauze swabs
carefully from the limb. I was very disturbed to observe the
extent to which it was reduced. The swabs had absorbed most
of the debris, and what was left was smaller than the tip of my
little finger; it was like the whole head of my limb had been
sucked away. It now resembled a sharpened pencil, except
that the grey lead of the pencil was the pink head of my limb.
There was still some yellowness at the tip. Nurse Know-It-
All dipped a swab in saline water with her gloved hand and
wiped the remaining debris from the head. I wished she'd be
quicker to cover it with the swab she was buttering with that
marmite thing, for it was getting more pitiable by the minute.

I saw that my circumcision, by contrast, was perfect – completely healed. It had a healthy pinkness to it and was no longer painful. It just felt as if I had been tightened with wire around it. I suppose it was the new and old skin growing into each other naturally. Rain had been right, I thought; I'd almost been a man in less than four days. It would have been a world record, had things not gone wrong the way they had.

19

I never did find out exactly what had caused my penis head to go rotten, but it is probable that during my work with the goatskin, I was too diligent about tightening the thong. This possibly caused the blood supply to the head to be cut off, and so gangrene set in. If I had been properly supervised, and assigned an experienced attendant the way I should have been, the problem could have been corrected and remedied long before it reached the stage it did.

Being in hospital as a patient is no joke, I can tell you that. It is not too different from being in prison, for those of us who have had the privilege of both. In hospital, like in prison, your life is not your own. You never know what to expect, what treatment will be meted out to you, especially if you are admitted for failed circumcision. You're never sure whether it's better to stay where you are or go back where you came from. Life seems worse either way.

While I lay there uncomfortably in the knowledge of being a patient, I was beginning to think about life outside as well. Nurse Know-It-All had told me I was doing fine. In fact, I was probably going to be discharged in another day or two. At first, I'd received this piece of information with delight. But the head people soon regained their grasp on things and saw my discharge in a different light. What it actually meant was that I was going to be released to the circus; everyone and anyone would poke fun at me for my deformity, throw insults at me for the scandal I'd caused and ostracise me for my apparent weakness. I knew this from the reactions I had already received from Grandfather, Mr Ugly the porter and Nurse Yaziyo.

I held onto the hope that Yanda, at least, would welcome me back. She would understand that what had happened to me was neither my fault nor my failure, and she would stand by me when no one else did. We would go off together to Wits, where I would take refuge. I would arm myself with education, become the intimidating lecturer type and overawe everyone with my superior status. Maybe I would write my research paper on the shortcomings of the male circumcision ritual as practised by the people of my tribe. In particular, I would expose the lack of care from the very parents who then argued that we rubbished their valued culture. I would show that it was men like Grandfather who, in fact, betrayed their own culture. They accused us of wrongdoing and called us "fragile", but it was due to their negligence that aftercare complications like mine occurred in the first place. It was because of the sins of our fathers that initiates like me ended up with permanent trauma; robbed of the respect of our community and ostracised by our society as men who weren't real men.

All of this I would point out in my research exposé. All of this I would have the courage to do if Yanda stood by me, like the friend I hoped she was.

I couldn't even begin to contemplate the alternative. If the Wits mission with Yanda did not materialise, I had no idea what I would do. What was clear to me was that I couldn't stay on at the village, where everyone now knew me as a failed man. But returning to Cape Town, to my father's shack, wasn't an option either.

It was at this point that a comforting thought crept up on the head people. I closed my eyes and stared into the vision they presented. It was a picture of whiteness. In this place, where I was aiming to get to, everything was white, just like in the hospital. The sky was covered with white, soft clouds. The air was so gentle it was less than a breeze. The place was populated by faces I didn't recognise, their bodies covered in white garments. They smiled at me, their eyes and teeth glowing. Even the ground was covered with white and pink flowers. Their fragrance lingered as I walked through them to find my bed, where I could have my eternal and comfortable sleep. I was just drifting off into it when I was brought back by the voice I loathed.

'Grains, *madoda*,' it yelled, intruding on my white-drenched fantasies. Nurse Know-It-All brought my food on a brown tray. She dumped it down on the trolley table and shoved it up to me. I was damn hungry, but I was not interested in that food: white rice, green peas, pumpkin and a chicken wing. My craving was for yellow maize grains served in a tin can on the mountain. Whatever appetite I had was further stolen away by the manner in which Nurse Know-It-All served the meal. There was just no compassion, you know?

Let me tell you, in my situation I wanted to be dealt with tenderly. I needed above all to be loved, cared for, understood. Nurse Know-It-All just wasn't that kind of nurse.

'Haven't you finished yet? I want to take your drip out,' she said to me in her loud way, so that the whole ward overheard.

'Do it...' I answered hoarsely.

I hadn't spoken out loud in a long time. All the debates I'd been having were with the head people in the confines of my skull. Now, when I uttered something, the words stumbled on my tongue and my voice came across grumpier than I'd intended.

Nurse Know-It-All went outside and came back with a trolley. There was cotton wool, scissors and plaster on it, just those three things. I don't know why she needed a whole damn trolley for only those three things. What is it with hospitals and trolleys? Everything gets brought with a trolley:

food, medicine, limbs, corpses, babies and what have you.

I never realised before that it is so much more painful to
remove a drip than to insert it. The most agonising part was
when Nurse Know-It-All ripped the plaster from the skin of
my hand. Shit! The damned thing must have pulled a million
hairs out of my skin. This is how our grandparents must have
felt when their pubic hair was removed with pliers in the
apartheid prisons.

After she left, I covered my whole head and body with the
sheet and tried to zone back into my white fantasy. At first
it was blurry and vague. But it grew whiter and clearer the
longer I focused on it. I tried to imagine the easiest way to
take myself there. Hanging myself was what first came to
mind, but it wasn't a very attractive option. For one thing, I
was sure it would be painful. For another, there was always
the possibility of being found at the crucial moment, or of the
rope snapping. Another blunder; no! I mean, I'd learnt from
Uncle's mistakes.

Then I remembered that there was this thing called *Dead-
line*, which was a poison they used to fumigate ticks and other
pests from livestock. Grandfather had a whole bottle of it.
He'd once demonstrated to us how strong the poison was by
pouring a teaspoonful onto a green enamel mug. It took less
than a minute for the pint to lose its greenness and become
just black metal.

I decided I was going to help myself to Grandfather's bottle.
It was the only thing I knew for sure would send me straight
into the bliss of whiteness. I folded the idea and packed it
safely away in the memory faculty of the head people... to be
continued.

Just after supper Nurse Know-It-All came in for the final
time, at the end of her shift, to say her goodbyes to the two *ma-
jugs*, for whom she seemed to have developed a fondness. As
always, there was no response from them. She knocked her
spectacles back into position and shuffled herself out again,

leaving the usual silence behind her, along with the sense of relief that her departure always gave.

It wasn't long afterwards that my beautiful night nurse came in to greet us. The head people drummed for joy at the sight of her. I felt the same way I used to feel when my brother came to the hut – comforted and cared for. The perpetual shame that engulfed me tucked its tail between its legs and returned to its handler.

'Good afternoon, *madoda*,' our nurse said in her soft and soothing voice.

'Afternoon...' Shorty, Tall and I answered in a chorus.

She made her way from bed to bed, smiling as always. Then her eyes landed on me and her smile seemed to grow more radiant, dimples forming in her cheeks. When she leaned over me, my nose caught the pleasant scent of the face powder she wore. It smelt the way I imagined her soul would: sweet.

'It seems we are doing well this evening, are we not?' she said to me.

I liked the way she referred to me as "we", as if she understood me from the inside. She was the exact opposite of Know-It-All, caring and gentle the way a nurse should be.

'We are doing fine, sister,' I said. 'Thank you.' But my voice didn't sound convincing, even to me.

There was silence while she continued to look at me. Her chest people must have had a conversation with mine, because she seemed to guess something of what I was feeling.

She came to stand at the head of my bed and without saying a word, gave me her hand to hold. Her touch was warm and soft. I felt her heartbeat throbbing in the blue veins of her hand. The chest people climbed with haste from the chest to the Adam's apple. I swallowed and swallowed, trying to force them down again, but in vain. I was incredibly grateful for the amazing show of kindness from this nurse who hardly knew me.

She continued to stand there, holding my hand and

squeezing it wordlessly. Without warning, I found my tears dripping down. Then I was weeping the way I hadn't wept since I was a boy. They were the first tears I had shed since my ordeal on the mountain had begun.

20

The next day, without warning, I was discharged. Such is life at the hospital – the House of Ruin, as some prefer to call it. Your fate is dependent on other people's whims and you have no say in things. If the doctors feel like it, you will be discharged. But if they aren't impressed with your prognosis you may develop bedsores on your buttocks, an indication that you have overstayed your welcome at the House of Ruin.

Fortunately, it didn't get that ugly for me. Apparently, Dr "Hey Buddy" had scribbled in my folder that I could be released that day, since my situation had now stabilised. He was the same guy who had examined me on the night I was brought in. At the time, he'd introduced himself to me by his proper name, but I was too preoccupied to take notice. I remembered his pale hands, brown shoes and khaki pants, but not his name.

I couldn't even make it out from the folder notes. Dr Hey Buddy's signature was impossible to read. It was easier to decipher Nurse Know-It-All's handwriting, in which she'd written the most trivial things about me and my situation.

'The patient is happier. This morning he greeted the nurse. He washed his own body. The caring nurse changed his linen, took out his IV and redid his dressing. Normal saline was used to clean the wound. The caring nurse observed that his wound is nice and pink. The patient ate his food, took his meds and went to pass stools once. He says his stools are hard and brown. He is mobile and tends to stand by the window a lot and stare outside. He is shy and doesn't speak much. By: E. Know-It-All, A/N.'

I recalled noticing something else under Nurse Know-It-All's notes, written in Dr Hey Buddy's cursive scrawl and signed with his impossible signature. But I hadn't paid too much attention. I'd long since given up trying to make sense of those illegible scribbles. I wasn't supposed to be fiddling with the folder in the first place.

It was only when my night nurse came in for her shift that evening that I learnt that I was, in fact, discharged, and had been since that morning already. That had been the indecipherable instruction scribbled by Dr Hey Buddy on my folder. I didn't know whether to be glad or sad about it. I was all mixed up inside.

My final day in hospital had begun no differently from the two before it. It had been dominated by the usual screams of our silence in the ward, broken periodically by deep burdened sighs and the restless twisting and turning of defeated warriors. There were long hours spent staring at the head people for answers that never came. These were interrupted only by Nurse Know-It-All's rough ministrations, and the twice-daily ordeal of visitors' hour.

Under normal circumstances, when you are in hospital there is nothing you wish for more than a visit from a relative or friend. I am not exaggerating when I say that the recovery of a patient partly depends on the number of visits he or she gets during the stay in hospital. It is the same when you are in prison or initiation school. How soon you overcome the trying times can depend on how many visitors you receive, and how frequently they visit you. Visitors are healers, see. Though they may be oblivious to this fact, they bring with them spiritual healing and a sense of acceptance for the one whom disaster has struck. So you look forward not to the

doctors' rounds, but the next visiting hour. This was not true
in my situation, however. For when you are an initiate who
has absconded from the mountain to turn yourself in at the
hospital, visitors are your worst nightmare. You dread them
like witchcraft.

The night before my discharge, I'd had an unpleasant dream
about just such unwelcome visitations. Earlier that evening,
our night nurse had invited us to come and watch television
in the ward next to ours. This turned out to be the nurse's
tea room cum rest room. It's where the Know-It-Alls of this
world ate their lunch, smoked, gossiped and slept. We sat
on the dirty couches while our nurse tuned the television set
to the *Simunye* channel. I saw the face of the legendary news
reader, Noxolo Mthimkhulu, reading the news with a level of
vernacular fluency most of us could only envy.

'In local news,' she said, 'the chairperson of the Eastern Cape
House of Traditional Leaders was extremely disappointed
that a new bill called the Application of Health Standards
in Traditional Circumcision was promulgated by parliament
yesterday. Rejecting the bill, the chairperson said: "We
cannot allow women, particularly those that are breastfeeding,
to fiddle with our boys' genitals... They can put me in jail, but
I'm not going to compromise on that. I will be the first to defy
this promulgation next week, when my youngest son goes to
the mountain...".'

The *Simunye* journalists had then gone to get the opinion
of the acting MEC for Health, who said the chairperson
was a chauvinist who led a mob of sexists who rejected
environmental change. He elaborated: 'There are numerous
men who were circumcised by female medical personnel in
hospitals, and they are men amongst us today. I wonder what
your chauvinistic chief will say to that!'

Noxolo Mthimkhulu went on to talk about the numbers
of youths who had died or whose genitals had had to be
amputated because of "complications" since the start of

the current circumcision season. She said that under the provisions of the new Act, 87 youths had been "rescued" from unsavoury initiation schools in Mthatha and elsewhere, and 20 traditional surgeons and attendants had been arrested. Septicaemia, dehydration and physical assault were the leading complaints of the initiates. The perpetrators were due to appear in court soon. They faced a fine of up to 10,000 rand, or ten years in jail.

I don't know about Shorty and Tall but my blood was boiling as I sat on that couch listening to Noxolo announcing the shame of our circumcisions gone wrong to the whole world. I cringed as I watched the 87 initiates with their white-smeared faces, knobkerries and blankets being frogmarched to the wards, while a mob of bearded faces in blue overall coats was bundled into the rear of police vans.

What really made me sick was the knowledge that the real problem would not be addressed by the current interventions, well-intentioned though they were. So long as our parents faltered, so long as the supposed custodians of our customs did not care for our well-being the way they were supposed to, and kept getting away with it, the government could try what it liked but the problem would only get worse.

Take my case, for example: I had done everything by the book. I had gone for the required blood test and got my circumcision licence. Geca himself was a licensed traditional surgeon, well-respected at his trade. I followed all the right procedures at the mountain. But there I was in hospital all the same, lying side by side with those whose paths may have been faulty in the first place.

I know I risk sounding like a broken record here, and if it seems like I am putting the blame for what happened at my grandfather's door, then it's because I am. There is no doubt in my mind that if he had taken the interest he was supposed to, I would not have experienced the suffering I did, and I would be a man today.

The news story obviously preyed on my mind, for that night I dreamed that the *Simunye* crew arrived at our ward. I was standing next to the window, staring out at the distant view of the rocky mountain when I heard a voice I recognised as Nurse Know-It-All's:

'Please, Son of God, don't disturb these two. They are too traumatised by their situation, I beg you,' she said.

I turned around and found her standing next to the beds of the two *ma-jugs*, who lay completely covered with their blankets as always. There was a man with bushy hair holding a huge camera on his shoulder. He was wearing a white *Simunye* T-shirt with the words "*Ons Is Een*" written across it. He was following a woman who carried a microphone in one hand and a small notebook in the other. She was wearing a black *Simunye* T-shirt with "*We Are One*" on it.

Nurse Know-It-All stood blocking their way towards the two *ma-jugs*. I saw Shorty and Tall shield their faces with their pillows and flee from the room with the camera guy in hot pursuit. I didn't move.

'What is your name, sir?' asked Miss Simunye, coming to stick the mic in my face. Her face was heavily made up and she smelled like a pink flower. Mr Simunye was back in the room again, busy angling me from all sides with his weapon.

'Uhm, I would like to remain anonymous, Miss Simunye,' I said.

'That's fine, sir. Could you just tell us why you are here, perhaps?'

'Well, I could... if I knew who you were, first of all...'

'I'm sorry for that, sir; I'm Lwimi Nondaba and this here is Chwephesha Gqwesile, and we are from *Simunye* TV. We would like to ask you a few questions about your stay here, and, most importantly, what brought you here, like,' said Miss Simunye.

At that point, the morning trolley came rumbling into my dream.

'*Mkhwetha!*' yelled Nurse Know-It-All's voice.

'*Mkhwetha!*'

I was rudely woken by the real Know-It-All, just when I was about to answer Miss Simunye's provoking questions. I was going to tell her the truth about the situation, that pure negligence was to blame for this alarming crisis that was affecting our culture. That the real root cause of the escalating infection and death rate among the young initiates was the lack of care, and abdication of responsibility, among those whose job it was to properly supervise their coming into manhood. Yes, that's what I would have told the *Simunye* team if Nurse Know-It-All hadn't interrupted when she did.

I got up, unsatisfied. My participation in the day's activities was passive and sluggish. I kept looking at the door, half expecting, even hoping, that the *Simunye* crew would rock up at the ward. They didn't, of course.

Someone else rocked up instead.

It was past three in the afternoon, the dreaded visitors' hour. The families of Shorty and Tall had come to see them, bringing fruit and something that smelled like fried fish. Each in turn went out the ward to have his private moment with his family in the rest room next door. As usual, I was relieved not to have recognised any of the visitors' faces. It was bad enough that the villagers knew that I was there, in the House of Ruin. I didn't want the word to spread further.

'Which one, sister?' I heard a man's voice saying in the corridor.

'Number six.'

'*Enkosi,*' the man said in thanks.

I wished I could communicate my dislike of visiting hours to the other patients, so that they would stop their visitors from wandering about and getting lost in the wards. I feared the possibility of encountering someone who knew me. The last thing I wanted was to be seen in a blue gown when I was supposed to be out on the mountain looking like an animal.

'There you are, *mkhwetha*,' said Sbenga's son, walking into the ward.

I looked at him in dismay while a jumble of thoughts chased each other around my skull. *What was he doing here? Had he come to pick me up? Or to spy on me? Had he perhaps been sent by mother to check how I was doing?*

'How is *mkhwetha*?' he asked.

'Fine.'

'Oh, fine.'

There was silence.

I was sitting on my corner bed, staring at the floor, while Sbenga's son appraised me, my bed, the *ma-jugs*, the whole ward. He held the van keys in his hand and sat fiddling with them. It became clear to me in that long moment of silence that he hadn't been sent by mother, or to pick me up, but was there to spy on me. He had come to get enough data to fill in the missing gaps in the gossip that I imagined was doing the rounds in the village. When he'd brought me here three days ago, he'd volunteered to wait by the car and not come in. But I'd seen in his face that it was against his will. He'd been hoping Grandfather would say he should come in with us, so that he could see what was done to me and tell the whole damn village when he got home. But since he had missed his chance then, I imagined that he must have been pressured by his friends to come and observe my progress.

I was annoyed.

'So, *mkhwetha*, when do they say you might come out?'

'I don't know.'

At that stage I still didn't realise I'd been discharged. I wanted to ask, 'Why is it important, anyway? Why, in fact, are you here?' But I simply shrugged and hid in silence.

'I see,' he said.

That's what Sbenga's son said: 'I see'. His words confirmed to me that he was, indeed, here to see, and that he had just told me so.

More silence.

'You must be wondering why I am here, *mkhwetha*. Sbenga sent me to deliver some cabbages at the evangelist's house here in Whittlesea. I remembered that I'd brought *mkhwetha* down here and thought it only right to pay him a visit. Delivering *mkhwetha* here was not to abandon him.'

'Okay,' is all I managed.

Sbenga's son looked at his wristwatch.

'The time is eaten by a dog, *mkhwetha*,' he said, and with that he left.

I was glad to see him go, not realising I would be seeing him again just a few hours later. This time, he was with Grandfather and they had come to pick me up.

The first I knew of my discharge was when my beautiful smiling night nurse came in to greet us that evening. Again, I was struck by the way she brightened our ward with her mere presence, as if the warmth of her nurse's "lamp" radiated out from her soul.

'So, we are going home tonight, then,' she said, studying the top page in my folder.

'Are we?' I said in surprise.

'Yes. Your doctor, Hey Buddy, has written here that the patient can be discharged. In fact, you were discharged this morning already. Nurse Yaziyo has noted that your grandfather has been phoned to come and collect you.'

She closed the folder and came to stand beside my bed, taking hold of my hand. Her warmth and empathy brought my tears down. She put her arms around me and held me against herself for a moment. Her hug was the most comforting embrace I'd felt in a long time.

'Take care of yourself, Lumkile,' she said to me. A last look, a last squeeze of my hand and she went out.

I thought she was going to come back later to say a proper goodbye. My eyes kept going to the door, expecting her to walk in again; right up to the moment that Grandfather came, I kept hoping. But she didn't appear.

I found myself struggling with tears as I hopped out of the hated gown and covered myself with the familiar stained blanket instead. I retrieved my leather thong from the drawer and walked out into the corridor, as friendless as I'd walked in. I didn't even say goodbye to my ward mates, Shorty and Tall; they were in the rest room again with their visitors. The two *ma-jugs* lay unmoving as always with their faces covered, like dead people.

As I followed Grandfather down the corridor, my head turned this way and that, still looking for my night nurse. It felt like I was leaving the one friend I had in the world. I realised I didn't even know her name. The chest people ached at the knowledge that I would never see her or the rest of the hospital staff again. I even found myself wishing to see Nurse Know-It-All one final time.

I followed Grandfather out of the brightness of the hospital and entered the darkness of the night, barefoot. Sbenga's son was waiting by the Hilux van, parked in the same spot as when he'd dropped me off.

My two enemies and I drove in silence to the village. What would happen next, what awaited me when we reached our destination, I had no idea. All I could think about was the five remaining stones around the fireplace at my hut; the concrete reminder that I hadn't made it as a man.

21

A drop of water pats me awake as it softly commits suicide on my forehead. I open my eyes and see that it drips from the zinc sheets above me. Pimple droplets are forming from the dew that has gathered there overnight. They are lining up on the zinc surface of my hut, aiming to die the silent death of water droplets.

I had come back here to finish what was unfinished. As soon as Sbenga's car had pulled up in the quiet of the sleeping village and released me, I had climbed back up in the dark to my abandoned hut.

Snippets of yellow come shooting in through the nail holes as the sun makes its way up from behind the mountain. My ears woke up to the concoction of noise drifting up from below. From this distance, the village sounds like a beehive; all the barks, bleats, bellows and crowing merged into a single, vibrating hum.

There is amazing softness under my left foot, smoother even than the powder of self-raising flour. What bliss, you might think. But don't be fooled. That deceitful softness will burn you. It is the softness of ash, the white and grey remains of the fire at the centre of the hut. There have been times when my foot accidentally dipped into that softness, only to burn from the still live red coals underneath it.

I retrieve some white rocks to make clay for the last time. Today it must be the thickest yet. I want to look like a proper goat. Everything must be done properly, today. It's the first time the men will see me on the mountain, and they are expecting to view for themselves the man who is flawed.

The raw clay is thick, soft and yellow. I apply it to my face with practised skill. Then I proceed to smear my whole body with it. When I say whole body, I mean exactly that; even my penis is painted yellow. The thick clay dries on my skin and becomes dazzling white. It feels like I'm wearing a diving suit.

I am full of trepidation for what lies ahead. Today is meant to be my big day, my triumphant exit into the community as a fully-fledged man. At last I am leaving this place. But I feel no triumph. I don't want to go home. I don't want to face what is waiting for me there.

I realise for the first time how scared I am. My deepest fear is that I can't trust myself. There is so much anger and hurt inside me. I have no control over my own feelings, and that makes me dangerous. I'm like a wounded beast that might lash out and injure, or even kill. At this moment, I just don't know what I'm capable of, what amount of damage I might cause to anyone who provokes me.

An idea strikes me: I need to do something metaphoric. Something that will warn my enemies and hint to them my dangerous state of mind. I will inscribe my cold-war declaration on the wall of the hut for all to see. I will use some of the clay to paint my message.

The head people storm with ideas and a litany of statements plants itself inside my skull. Which one will it be? All Eyes On Me? Me Against The World? Things Fall Apart? End of The Road? A Better Life for All?

None of them seems right. Then, like a thief, a remembered mission statement creeps in unannounced, and there it is: "These Are All Sins of My Own". Bold and precise; or is it? Is it true that today I am who I am because of my own sins? Am I the failure of my own making? Or does all of this flow from the sins of the fathers?

It is around midday when I witness a mob of male figures marching like soldiers to my hut. My eyes pick out a hellish darkness hanging above them, as if they are accompanied by a shadow of death.

I had been sitting on the top of my hut like a baboon, the sun baking my back while I waited for them. I'd been anticipating their coming since mid-morning. Now, here they were. They looked like an army coming to evict me. There were so many of them, the whole damn village, it seemed. Everyone was wanting to see for himself what I had become, wanting to be part of the historic event of taking the failed man home. They were all so eager to be part of my downfall, but where had they been earlier? Why hadn't they come when they were needed, to do the work of guiding me?

Ordinarily, they would have been singing proudly and stick fighting as they approached. I should have heard women's ululation and singing, too. But today seemed like a burial day in the village. Mournfulness weighed the air.

I heard Uncle's voice from within the mob, ringing out with excitement. He was carrying a big bundle wrapped in a brown blanket, balanced on his knobkerrie. I read the aggression in the crowd and my heart beat faster. I noticed there were a lot of dogs with them. It was unusual for the men to have so many dogs with them on an occasion like this. It was almost as if they were coming to hunt, not escort me down.

It is customary for the initiate to run into his hut as soon as he notices the men approaching. He must always be found inside. Men, real men, don't do manly business in the street. They must be in the confines of a kraal, the makeshift kraal in this instance being my hut and I being the host, the head of the household. But I was not in the mood for pretentious protocol. It didn't matter anymore what I did right or wrong since nothing was going to redeem this situation. In fact, what I was hoping for was for someone to challenge me. I had a lesson to teach anyone who dared to suggest I wasn't a proper man. I had my knobkerrie and my axe, too, if I needed it. All I wanted was one man who would be man enough to give me an excuse to use it.

My dog sensed trouble. Its tail was up, its ears erect. I was glad I'd remembered to unchain it earlier that morning. It looked at me for instruction, then back at the advancing crowd in utter distrust. That look! It seemed to be saying, 'I'm ready when you are'. The grimacing smile hardened on my face. It dawned on me that there is a reason why people say dogs are man's best friend.

About eight giant dogs came sprinting towards the hut the minute they saw my dog. They were coming to attack him. I jumped off the roof of the hut, the chest people beating fast with a mix of anger and anxiety. Someone was hailing, calling the dogs back. His voice was not insistent enough. If I was a dog, I would think he was cheering me on. That's why the dogs went dog instead.

My dog gave me that look again; this time there was fear in his glassy eyes. He was scraping the dust, causing turmoil with his hind legs while he made heart-breaking moans. Urine dripped from his member. He was calling me to his defence. He did not know what I was planning. He was not aware that the chest people were wishing with all their might that these dogs would dare to attack him, so that I could teach them a lesson they wouldn't forget. It seemed that I would get my wish, for the dogs were determined. To them, I didn't exist. All they saw was him, their victim. I tightened my grip on the knobkerrie and waited for them to come in range.

As I did so, I had a sudden memory of the day I'd killed my first rabbit. I remembered walloping it between the eyes, and the sight of it afterwards, looking like it had been run over by a 16-wheel truck. The skull had been completely crushed by that single blow. I recalled the pride I'd felt then, and thinking: *Damn, but I am deadly with this stick!* Now, as the dogs covered the distance towards us, that memory encouraged me. The difference was that today I wasn't going to harm a rabbit but a dog – and its handler, if it came to that.

I called for my dog to sit down. It came to hide between my legs, its tail tucked under. The other dogs came on at full speed, Sbenga's dog leading the pack. I did not move. Sbenga's dog was a beautiful dog, creamy white, speckled with black spots. I don't know whether it did not notice me standing there in my white-smeared make-up, or simply did not give a fuck. It had outrun the other dogs by a good few metres and was coming straight for us, its tongue dangling hungrily and its sharp canines at the ready. I heard a voice from the crowd calling to the dog, trying to divert it from its mission. But the dog went dog.

I had thought it would go for my dog and was taken by surprise when it jumped for me instead. I shifted to the side and walloped it with my knobkerrie. It was so heavy it was like bringing down something massive, like attempting to throw a bag of cement down with one hand. It crash-landed on its back against the zinc and lay there, wailing horribly.

Let me tell you, the wailing of an injured dog is worse than the screaming of a woman who has lost her firstborn. It is the kind of wailing that remains echoing between your ears for years afterwards. Sbenga's dog never regained its mobility. I saw it a few days later when I was on my way home from the dam. Its white body was hanging, lifeless, in the same pine tree from which my uncle had once tried to hang himself. As people said, Sbenga did the honourable thing by hanging it. He could not watch it suffer any longer. As for me, I had to live with the guilt of paralysing a dog. That guilt is still with me, years later.

My dog now ran into the hut. It did not seem to notice that the rest of the dogs had come to a screeching halt once I'd dealt with their frontrunner. My blood had reached boiling point and I was blind and deaf to everything but my rage. I went for the rest of the dogs laying about me with my knobkerrie. I must have looked fearsome because each tucked its tail under and headed back to its handler. I would have followed them and gone for the handlers, too, if I had not seen my dog speed past me, chasing the other dogs. I was quick to call it back, for I was worried those bastards might kill it.

I returned to the top of my hut with a boldness that surprised me. Sbenga's dog was trying to lift itself up, heaving its paralysed body helplessly and falling from side to side. It was still wailing and wailing. The men had stopped at a distance, all looking at the dog. I could hear their angry voices.

'He has hurt the dog!'

'Hurt? He has cut the damn dog in half!'

'It's paralysed!'

'What kind of a man wastes a dog like this!'

'Sbenga will cripple him too!'

Then a voice I recognised as my uncle's said: '*Madoda*, since when do you mind a fight between two dogs? A dog is a dog is a dog. Dogs fight each other every day. Dogs have ripped each other's testicles since I was a young boy. I say again, what is new in a fight between two dogs?'

That's what he said, my uncle. My own flesh and blood was calling me a dog.

The crowd fell silent at his words. My uncle then said something to the small boys in the crowd. They separated from the men, lagging behind while the mob of men continued to walk towards my hut. When they were about two hundred metres away, my uncle yelled for me.

'*Mkhwetha?*'

I knew what was expected of me but I wasn't prepared to respond, especially not to him. I mean, he knew how abruptly we had parted on our last encounter and he surely wasn't expecting me to be dishonest about it. I could feel my face cramped into a crazy grin, my blood raging.

I was still trying to figure out what was going on here. The biggest question in my head was this: *Did Sbenga's dog attack me out of its instinct or... was it set on me deliberately?*

I needed an immediate answer to this question. The head people were determined that either I got my answer or I died seeking it. The first one from that crowd to come close to me was going to know all about it. Today the expected ululation was going to be replaced with wails. And I wasn't going to be one of the wailers, of that I was certain.

I tightened and loosened my grip on the knobkerrie, clenched and unclenched my teeth, crossed and re-crossed my legs as I sat on top of my hut, waiting.

If you haven't been through what I have, my reactions might seem extreme. Let me just say that on that day, I literally feared for my life. I was an outcast in my community, the object of scorn and scrutiny. My failure was not only mine, but the culture's. This made people angry because they held their culture and practices so dearly. They saw me as the bad apple, projecting a negative impression of what they're made of. I just didn't know what to expect out there on the mountain, and the mood of the crowd led me to believe that anything might happen. Nothing was as it should be. For one thing, Grandfather wasn't there. He was supposed to set fire to the hut and burn it. But he hadn't even come.

The crowd came to a halt a good few metres away, as it dawned on them that I wasn't answering any of their calls. Uncle motioned that they should wait there. A hundred years went by. Then two men emerged out of the crowd and made their way towards me. I jumped down, swinging the knobkerrie with intent, the head people already calculating the number of steps it would take me to reach my axe if my knobkerrie failed me.

Then I saw who the two men were, and my knees suddenly turned to jelly, followed by the rest of my body. They were *Ta*'Yongs and Rain. I felt completely betrayed. Those were the last two I had been expecting to see among that hostile mob.

I slid into my hut, the wells behind my eyes overflowing

with rage and despair. *Ta'*Yongs and Rain came inside and sat down. They didn't greet me, they simply sat and stared at me while I battled with the flood drenching my eyelashes and muddying the clay on my face.

*Ta'*Yongs reached slowly towards his hip and pulled out a handgun. It was black and shiny, and I don't know why but the head people registered it as a deadly scorpion. He pressed something and a magazine slid out. He held it so that I could see the bullets loaded in there. Then he slid it back and cocked the weapon. He stood half bent and shoved the gun back into the holster on his hip. The grin cramped my face vigorously. It was like I was developing a stroke or something.

'You are safe, *ndoda*. Take your blanket and let's go,' *Ta'*Yongs said.

'You have no business in this place any more. This man and I are here for one purpose only: to deliver you safely to your mother.'

My mother? Had she then asked them to come?

I did as I was told. But before I could make my way out of the hut, *Ta'*Rain said something I will never forget.

'Remember this, *mkhwetha*: from today, you are a man in your own right. That's all I will say to you.'

Those words vibrated between my ears: I'm a man in my own right... my own right... right... a man... man... in my own right... I covered my whole body with the blanket and hid my head from everyone as I was meant to do. I wish I could remember the bearded faces I was met with as I emerged from my hut. I recall the distaste in those faces, and the jokes that had them giggling among themselves, but not the faces themselves. I was too dizzied by the suddenness with which things had switched. I'd surprised myself when I'd surrendered so quickly to these two men. I'd had to jump in an instant from one extreme state to the other. The head people were all in a whirl, busy wondering what would have happened had *Ta'*Yongs and Rain not been there to rescue the situation. The wailing of that dog!

'Come, this side... yes,' said Rain, as he lowered the fence for me to get through. We were now heading for Ox-Kraal dam. The men were behind me, and someone was leading them as they began to sing *Somagwaza*. I knew full well that the only reason they were there was to see my penis for themselves and confirm the rumours about it. Hearsay wasn't a good enough option in such a scandalous story. They would have chewed my defecation if I'd asked them to, so long as that would have enabled them to view my penis. Never in my life had my genitals received so much attention.

'I'm going to tell you when to run,' Rain said. 'I hope you know a good place where you can wash thoroughly. You must listen to me when I tell you to throw the blanket down and run. Never look back, you hear? Never. Even if your penis falls down don't turn your head. A man does not do that. You will not be bothered by the young boys chasing you today. You scared them shitless. You are going to run at your own pace. When we get to you we must find you thoroughly clean. I don't want anyone touching you, but if you don't wash thoroughly I'll be forced to let them. You don't want that. From there, we go straight home. Are you ready?'

'Yes...'

'*Lahla, mkhwetha!*'

I threw the blanket off as soon as I heard Rain's command.

I ran as fast as I could, even though no one was chasing me. Ordinarily, the small boys would have run behind me with sticks, taking the opportunity to chase the initiate away from boyhood into manhood. But my unpredictable behaviour had alarmed everyone, and the boys had been warned to keep away from me.

And so, I chased myself into manhood.

I'd hardly even run a hundred metres but already I was panting like a dog. I was still very weak from the trauma that my body had gone through, and the stay in hospital had sapped my strength further. The shores of Ox-Kraal bladder were still far off. I suddenly tasted bitterness at the back of my tongue. I was salivating, and yellowness stole my vision. I just made it to the shores of the dam, where I knelt and threw up the contents of my stomach. My vomit was nothing more than gastric acids and saliva, for I hadn't eaten that morning. It left a foul taste in my mouth. Mucus and tears followed, and there was jelly in my joints as I entered the pool.

The water was warm. It had turned coffee brown from the recent rains. I waded to the spot where I knew there was a flat stone to stand on and felt the ooze of mud between my toes.

The men caught up and stood waiting in the shade of trees for me to come out. Uncle put down the load he carried, wrapped in the brown blanket. He searched for something and came up with a green brick.

'Here, *mkhwetha*,' he said. '*Sunlight* soap is good for animals. *Waa ga ga ga!*' The men all joined in his laughter. He added, scornfully, 'It's the same one they use to scrub horses with.' He broke the brick in half, then threw it to me. I moved my body aside and let the soap die an unnatural death in the water. It sank from sight. The crowd once again fell silent. I know I behaved like the teenager I was, throwing unwarranted tantrums, but in my head, I was fixing something.

*Ta'*Yongs took the remaining half of the soap from Uncle's hand. I locked my eyes with his. It's like our souls were in conversation. He waved the soap to me as if it was a chocolate bar, then threw it. This time I dived and caught the green brick. I smeared my whole body with it, noticing as I did so that my shaved pubic hair had already started to grow back.

The crowd of men abandoned their patches of shade and headed for the shore as soon as they saw me wading back towards it. The moment of truth had arrived; it was now or never for them to witness with their own eyes what they were so keen to see. The water was waist deep, then down to my knees, my ankles, and then I was out. Thanks to the cold, the limb in question had shrunk to its smallest ever. But that did

not interest anyone. What they wanted to see was whether I'd
been sutured on my circumcision. That was the biggest myth
sown into people's heads at the villages, that doctors suture
the circumcision and then smear it with *Betadine* antiseptic.
A sutured circumcision is not considered to be a real
circumcision, and such cases are contemptuously referred to
as '*oonotywetywe*' – *Betadine* men.

Rain threw me a yellow towel from Uncle's bundle. I have
no idea why my mother bought me yellow, of all things, since
it's considered to be a girl's colour. I dried myself with it
anyway. Then, as Rain was busy lotioning me with margarine,
he said:

'Don't you want me to... show them that it's not sutured,
mkhwetha? I mean, that is the only reason they are all here.
Let's disillusion them once and for all. Show them your
circumcision, rub it in their bearded faces that you're not a
bogus man. You are real.'

'Okay,' I said. I would have agreed to be re-circumcised all
over again if it was Rain who asked me.

'Look, *madoda*, it does not have even a bit of an ailment;
here it is... see for yourselves that this boy is now a man.'

Ordinarily, I should have witnessed celebratory smiles on
the men's faces. Someone should have burst into song at that
point, once they had seen for themselves that my manhood
wasn't flawed. Now, if any time, the stick fighting should have
begun. I regret to say that none of that happened. As with
Grandfather previously, disappointment grew on the bearded
faces. They didn't want to see for themselves that I was a man;
they wanted evidence of my failure. They wanted the zigzag
scars of sutures. Once again, I felt that piercing, stinging pain,
as if the chest people were being circumcised. That pain!

'Now we will take the route that goes past the graveyard,
church and river, and you will be home. Remember what I
told you: don't look back. I will teach you other things in the
house of the lamp tonight. Let us go,' said Rain.

It was Rain, in his high-pitched voice, who began the singing of *Somagwaza*. It was he, with his limp, who began challenging other men to a stick fight. Little by little, the excitement grew. It invigorated especially as we approached my home. Several pairs of stick fights broke out there, men accosting each other with their knobkerries, trying to impress the waiting women with their manly prowess. It was hard to believe these were the same men who had come to collect me. They were now so animated, singing *Somagwaza* like never before. They fought with their sticks until some of them were on the ground on their backs, fighting like cats.

At home, the mothers and girls were waving scarves and brooms, singing, ululating and dancing, blocking the men from entering. We had to earn our way in with our impressive fighting skills. My ears were divided between two songs: *Somagwaza* sung by the men and *Uzolile lamfana* by the women.

The voices of my mothers were soothing and that song, in particular, was pleasantly ironic. "*Uzolile lomfana*" can loosely be translated as "Oh the tranquillity of this young man". The ironic chorus goes something like this:

Wenza ngabom'
Sondela
Wenza ngabom'
Sondela
Wenza ngabom'
Sondela uzakuyibon'intoyakho.

'Oh the tranquillity of this young man, oh his harmony, his calmness. Don't be fooled, though, he's just pretending. He's doing it deliberately. Take a closer look and you'll see what he's really made of.'

So the song went on until we men earned our entry into the yard. The women then broke into sporadic ululation, standing on the periphery of the exuberant mob of fighting men. It's as if they let us win. You know how women do that; they let men deceive themselves with the notion that they are in charge of things.

Among all those women, there was one who was not wholly in this world. She did not join in any of the group songs. She wore a cream dress with faded flowers, and her face was hidden with a wide-brimmed straw hat. She stood with her arms lifted up like the horns of a Brahman cow, singing in her hoarse voice the song that could only be sung by her on an occasion like this one:

Ndiza'lubelek'usana lwam
'Lubelek'usana lwam
Ndine bhongo ngo sana lwam
Ndine bhongo
Ndiza'lubelek'usana lwam
'Lubelek'usana lwam

'I'm so proud of my baby, I have a good mind to put him on my back right now.'

That woman was my mother. She was overcome with not just excitement but awe.

After my long and lonely time of hurting and sadness, here was someone referring to me as her baby, telling everyone that even now, there was no reason why she could not still put me on her back. I had shed many tears of sorrow but at this moment came tears of joy. If I had any doubts about whether I should continue living or not, that was the moment when those doubts were laid to rest.

22

Because of all the other goings-on, it had escaped the notice of the head people that the day after my coming out was the same day the matric results were due to be released. Let me say that along with Nelson Mandela's birthday and New Year's Eve, the day of the matric results ranked top in order of importance in our village. It was the annual joke that even those who couldn't separate A from A still bought the newspaper that dispatched these important results on that day.

It was now mid-morning after the all-night celebration of my coming out and the head people were dancing between sleep and wakefulness. I waited for someone to bring me the news since I was not able to leave the house and go in search of it myself. I kept hoping that it would be Yanda. So far, I hadn't heard a word from her since my return from the mountain. She hadn't kept her promise to stay with me all through the night of my coming out. She hadn't come to the celebration ceremony at all.

The ceremony had been held the previous night at the house of the lamp, and I'd been mesmerised by what went down there. It's in the house of the lamp that *ikrwala*, the new man, hosts other unmarried men and women on a night vigil, celebrating his successful return from the mountain. Note the word "successful". It is only after he has gone through this rite that an initiate earns his rightful place in the house of men.

*Ta'*Yongs had said his goodbyes after ensuring that I arrived home safely from the mountain. He'd promised to see me the following day.

'I've left my number with your mother... phone me if there's any trouble, okay?' he'd said.

I was now left in the capable hands of Rain. One thing I was happy about was that Rain was not a drinker. He enjoyed his *amarhewu*, a beverage made from mealie meal, but that was all. He sat with me on the straw mat at the corner of the house of the lamp all through the night. It was he who accompanied me when I needed to go outside to urinate. He tucked my new brown blanket around me and walked me out to the sheep pen, where I released water. He turned out to be the aftercare attendant I never had.

Uncle kept coming over to where I was sitting, making unintelligible statements in his intoxicated state. These went unheeded. Although it was technically his house, he had no power over it tonight, since the space had become transformed into something else; it was *endlwini yesibane* – the house of the lamp.

It was past 10pm when Rain, the gentlemen's gentleman, asked for order in the house and opened the vigil officially.

'*Madoda*, I won't be tall,' he said in his welcoming speech.

He thanked all who were present for coming to honour me and for the good work done during the proceedings of the day, which included making sure that the sheep were slaughtered and cut up and firewood was chopped, and for bringing the initiate back safely.

'Lastly, I would like to thank all those men who volunteered themselves to go and request the ladies from their homes... thank you, *madoda*. And I want to say to the ladies especially, it is the honour of the initiate to have you here tonight. I urge you to stay in the house of the lamp until dawn. We did not request you from your parents so that you could disappear when you like. Do we hear each other? That said, *madoda*, and you ladies, of course, the rules of the house of the lamp are still the same: let us treat the house of the lamp like the house of the lamp. Without being tall, I would like to invite any man out of those who have already earned the right to speak in the house of the lamp to say a few words, and then we can proceed.'

'They are beautiful... cousin, your words are put beautifully...' Uncle was beginning to say, when he was cut short by Rain.

'First of all, this is not a house for cousins. Second, as someone who claims to be a man in the home of this initiate, and an uncle above all, you should be the one doing what I am doing right now. Having failed to do that, and with the amount of damage consequential to your failure to act manly, I would rather you swallowed your words before you expose your manliness or the lack of it to scrutiny, as the case may be. Now, if there is no one else who has something to say...'

'Over here Rain, *ntanga*. Over here,' said Nduku, another of Mother's many cousins.

Uncle fell silent at Rain's words and has remained that way to date, at least on matters that involve me. He simply has no say. 'Thank you Rain, *ntanga*,' said Nduku. 'I am also not intending to be tall. I just want to emphasise one point you touched upon briefly... about the ladies. I was one of those who vomited... volomited... vominteered to go and request these ladies from their parents. You are correct, *ntanga*, people have got a tendency to priterpret things wrongly. Ladies, we were sent by the house of the lamp to go and request your presence from your parents. We urge you to be mindful of that fact. We want your parents to allow you to attend the house of the lamp again next time. As I sit down, *ntanga*, I want to remind the ladies, and their bulls for that matter, that the punishments for disappearing from the house of the lamp have not changed. *Ntanga*, take your place.'

Rain took over again and, on my behalf, declared the house

of the lamp open. He then instructed: 'According to positions, *madoda.*'

Without further ado there was swift movement and changing of positions among the men sitting against the wall. There must have been about forty or fifty men in that room, all taking the positions assigned to them according to the strict codes of the house of the lamp. There were no chairs in the house of the lamp and the floor was bare, with only a thin layer of cow dung smeared on it. I noticed that the seating arrangements followed the order of seniority in circumcision – ranging from the most recently circumcised, to those who had gone to the mountain before some of us were even conceived. Everyone sat anxiously, not wanting to attract Rain's scrutiny, for his word was law here. There was also the suspense of wondering which lady he would assign to whom, and everyone was now eyeing everyone else with suspicion.

Silence fell on the house of the lamp.

The ladies were left standing behind the door, holding the "lamps", which were lit candles. Although I hadn't been particularly interested in the proceedings of the house of the lamp up to this point, knowing full well that it was all pretence since I was not considered to be a man in the eyes of many in that room, I was very curious as to what was to follow next.

Rain took his knobkerrie and walked from corner to corner, checking on the correct order of the seating arrangements in the house of the lamp. Everyone lifted their heads up so that they could be counted. All at once, those sullen faces I'd seen when they came to collect me from the mountain, that same hostile attitude, was back in the tension of Rain's scrutiny. The house of the lamp seemed to be running short of oxygen, for the penalty for error, for having taken up the wrong seating position, was high.

'Right,' Rain exclaimed, satisfied with the arrangements, and sighs of relief were heaved across the house. Then he added: 'To the lamps, ladies.'

Six of the ladies who stood against the door went to remove the remaining candles from the blue walls of the room, where they had been stuck with their own wax. The only source of light in the house was now held by the girls. All the brightness drifted towards the door where the ladies stood, leaving the rest of the house of the lamp in darkness. The only faces that could be seen were those of the ladies. They seemed to glow under the light, while the men were just stick figures in darkness.

Rain came to whisper in my ear. I couldn't believe what he was saying to me. Out of all those hungry beasts that filled the house of the lamp, he was asking me to be the one to choose first. He was giving me that honour. Trickles of pride massaged my soul. Then the head people recovered from their surprise and I answered 'No'. I thought I'd embarrassed myself enough already, see, and I wasn't ready to subject myself to more gossip. For one thing, I'd never been with a woman; I was still intact, remember! I wasn't really sure what was expected of me with a lady and I didn't want my first time to be here, in public. For another thing, there was the more scandalous matter of my unusual genitals.

'Are you sure?' Rain asked, disappointed. He knew that I had no girlfriend because I'd told him on the mountain, and he'd guessed that the initiate needed to be initiated.

'Yes, sure...' I told him. I wanted to add: 'But thank you for asking, like.'

Silence was still in order in the house of the lamp. The tension was palpable as men ejaculated carbon dioxide through their noses, waiting anxiously in the darkness for Rain to make his call. The ladies continued to stand in the unstable brightness of the candlelight, their beautiful shadows cast on the blue walls behind the door.

'Sindi,' Rain called out, 'follow me... open up Nduku... sit here, Sindi.'

Sindi went to sit between Nduku's legs as instructed. And I

couldn't care less if I "priterpreted" things slightly wrong, but it seemed Nduku was pleased beyond the word pleasure.

'Babsie... over there... with Zane.'

'Bullet, in that corner... with Ncukacha... no, no, pardon me, with Mbu, *ja*.'

Rain allocated all the girls to sit with the men he designated. Unfortunately, this was the only house where there were fewer women than men. The other unpalatable part was that if your girlfriend was allocated to sit between another man's legs, you had no say in the matter. You just had to take it like a man. What happens in the house of the lamp stays in the house of the lamp.

The candles burnt thinly from the corners, their brightness threatened by the heavy breathing of a roomful of horny men. Unstable dimness settled on the room. Nduku led the house of the lamp in evocative song. His baritone made the corrugated iron sheets of the roof tremble. This song was sung with such well-rehearsed orderliness it sounded like an opera. There was no dancing or ululation accompanying it. Rain circled the room, pausing above each head and listening to check that everyone was in tune, emphasising the important lyrics of the song for those who weren't singing them correctly and psyching everyone up to deliver their best baritone. Lamps fell one by one to the ground and they were plunged into the darkness of the night.

Rain came to stand over my head, singing the anthem of the house of the lamp and hammering the wall with his knobkerrie as he got me to master the right tone and lyrics. That was very helpful and... arousing, too. I was the only person in the room who did not know the song, since I was the newest member of the house of the lamp. After all, the purpose of the house of the lamp is to teach a returning initiate the manly things: how to be with a woman; the language of men; and other activities consequential to being a man. I repeated after Rain:

If a cat holds its tail up high
You must know it is wet on the posterior

If a cat holds its tail up high
You must know it is wet on the posterior

After repeating those lyrics over and over, my voice grew hoarse and my head spun as I was absorbed into the contagious mood of the darkness. I might not know what each bearded face was thinking in that darkness, but I am sure of one thing: each man was inadvertently nursing his hardness.

If a cat holds its tail up high
You must know it is wet on the posterior

My suspicion was confirmed first by the encounter between Nduku and Sindi, and later, others, too.

'Not you again, Nduku,' Sindi whispered.

'If a cat holds its tail up high, you must know it is wet on the posterior...'

'I can't be your cat again, Nduku!'

'If a cat holds its tail up high, you must know it is wet...'

'*Yhu*! Not again. This is the last time, Nduku. *Yhu*!'

'If a cat holds its tail up high...'

'Okay, *ke*. But this is the last...'

'If a cat holds...'

The night was a repetition of this and more. The candles were relit only twice, for a double round of food and drinks. I found it ironic that it should be called the house of the lamp, for the lamps disappeared or were made to disappear, during the hours of orgasmic darkness. It generally took hours to find another source of light, and when one was found, it was not much. But nobody cared.

If a cat holds...

The following morning, I was exhausted and spent, as if I'd been trying the whole night long to find out what happens if a cat holds its tail up high. Rain was now fast asleep on the straw mat beside me. One of us had to remain awake in case the elders, or "white heads" as they were known, came to the house of the lamp to "borrow" me for a talking to at my grandfather's kraal. We were expecting them to come any time between now and midday. This is the time when the grandfathers and other elderly men have their session with the returning initiate and give him all manner of commands and directives into adulthood. No matter how difficult I found it, I had to remain awake to wait for their summons, for our manhood, Rain's and mine, would be questioned had we been found sleeping at daylight.

The sound of a revving car outside reminded me that Mother should by now have sent someone to buy the newspaper in town. I felt frustrated that I was stuck at the house and couldn't go to get it myself. I wanted to open the paper with my own hands and check if my name was there. If you had passed, your name would be printed under the name of your school. An E next to your name meant you had got a university pass, and a D meant a pass with distinction.

Where was Yanda with the news? Where was she?

At that moment, I heard commotion outside. My mother, brother, sister, cousins and aunts came bursting into the house of the lamp as if they were being chased by bees. They were all screaming and yelling together:

'Your name is in the paper...'

'You have passed...'

'It's an exemption...'

'It's the only one from your school...'

It didn't matter at that moment that they weren't meant to enter the house of the lamp; we were all too excited to care. I'd thought that when I got the news I would jump up and down and run madly about with the paper in my hands like a championship trophy. I would frame it for my children to see. But I just sat there motionless, my body numb with excitement. I was being hugged, kissed, pulled and shoved from all directions in honour of my achievement. When I was a boy I was never able to hold my tears back if my mother cried. I couldn't hold them now.

'Where is the paper?' I asked.

My question was not so much to do with my own results, but Yanda's. I wanted to know if her name appeared, too. Did she also get an exemption, like?

'We've sent someone to town for the paper. You'll get it soon,' my mother said.

'So how do you know...?'

'Didn't you hear the car revving outside? That was your classmate, coming to bring the news. She was so happy for you, my child, she cried. She came here specially to show us your name... I saw it with my own eyes, *maan*. She said she'd collect your statement of symbols from the school and deliver it in person.'

'What was her name?' I asked, the chest people beating each other like drums.

'What did she say her name was again? *Thixo wam*... Yanga, wasn't it?'

'Yanda,' my brother corrected, 'her name was Yanda.' My mother nodded.

'And she was a natural beauty, *maan*; you must know her?' A smile developed on my face when I heard my mother describe Yanda as a natural beauty. Then the smile disappeared. 'Did her name... also appear in the paper?' I ventured to ask.

My mother's face fell.

'Oh bless that child. And God bless the woman who gave birth to her. She was crying, *mntanam*. She said "*Yho mama, krwala* will be so disappointed with me. The two of us had pledged to clinch university passes together. I have failed him. My name appeared but I did not get the university grades...".'

I sat there feeling cold, even though the sun was bright outside. My sense of elation of a few minutes before had evaporated. All I could think about was that Yanda hadn't made it. That was a shock for both of us.

I didn't have too much time to dwell on this, though, for soon after this the white heads arrived to "borrow" me from the house of the lamp. They were all very drunk, so much so that they could hardly stand. They sang *Somagwaza* with hung-over voices. There was no stick fighting. The women chanted vague ululations. It was generally a tired day.

Rain and a few men from the house of the lamp accompanied me to the kraal. I was covered in my new brown blanket, my face hidden from everyone. It was almost lunch time, and food was being cooked in huge three-legged pots over the fire at the centre of the kraal. The men would get meat and *samp* mealies, while the women cooked separately for themselves and the children in the house.

Just as in the house of the lamp, I noticed that the elders sat in order of seniority. But there were many complexities to the seating arrangements. It wasn't just physical age, but the age at which a man had been circumcised and got married that determined who sat next to whom. Sometimes, a younger man with schooling or well-off could be found sitting with the white heads without being questioned.

Now that I was seeing through a manhood lens, I could pick up subtleties that others might miss. It had been a great help that Rain had spent half the night teaching me how to interpret this new world, while the other men in the house of the lamp were busy finding out what happens if a cat holds its tail up high.

Rain spread the straw mat next to the white heads and helped me to sit down. Even a simple exercise like sitting down had to be done with absolute carefulness. Men, real men, don't throw themselves like kids onto the couch when they sit, they seat themselves grown-up style, with respect and honour. So, the way I conducted myself as I sat down, not showing my nakedness, for example, was an important observation for the elders. It would help to determine the way they would regard me for the rest of my life. These were the kind of intricacies that Rain was helping me to master.

Rain sat down next to me and put my new enamel dish in front of me. Then the elders came to toss coins into it, as they spoke one after the other.

'With these five cents, I say to you there must never be scarcity in this home,' said one white head.

'May you prosper,' said another, and I saw the smallest coin that ever existed being thrown into the dish.

'This is the foundation for your *lobola*. We won't give you the hands of our daughters without *lobola*. Here, before these giant men, I give you capital for your *lobola*. You shall not trouble your parents for cows for *lobola*.' With another "ting" a brass coin hit the enamel.

But all of this came only after Grandfather had made his contribution. Grandfather, the one man I couldn't even bear to look in the eye. True, looking elders in the eye was still forbidden to an initiate like me, but I'd at least stolen glances from behind my blanket at the other drunken faces. Grandfather, I could not bring myself to view at all. When he started to speak, I wished I could stuff my ears with cotton wool. I wasn't ready to listen to his hypocrisy.

He began with tears. The head people weren't impressed and advised me to think about something else, something more important than this insincere display.

I waited coldly for him to speak. What I was expecting from him was that he should at least speak honestly about what had happened, acknowledge the flaws that had occurred and, perhaps, apologise for failing in his responsibility. Apologise, if not to me, then to the other white heads. His kraal had brought shame to manhood itself, and now was an opportunity for him to address this. But when he did speak, all he said was: 'The lion! Mmh...'

That's exactly what he said, my grandfather: 'The lion!'

He took out a crumpled handkerchief from his brown blazer and wiped his tears away.

'You must see a hungry lion, mmh... it closes its eyes and lays its body in tall grass... you will think it is asleep... nooo!... A hungry lion does not sleep... it is not asleep, it is waiting for its prey. A real man is like a lion, child of my child, like a hungry lion.'

I suppose that for a drunken person there was some sense in what he said, but the head people were disgusted with such junk. Grandfather's speech about lions was relegated to the nonsense box of my skull, along with the speeches of the other drunken white heads. The words of wisdom they supposedly had for me amounted to nothing at all.

Once again it was left to *Oom* Dan to rescue the situation. He stood up and I saw the eyes of the other white heads following him expectantly as he approached the corner of the kraal where I was sitting with Rain. They were probably anticipating something poetic from him, for as a death announcer he was known for his well-crafted speeches. Dan stood there for a moment, leaning on his knobkerrie as he surveyed me through my blanket. Then he said: '*Ubudoda licebo, mfowam.* A man is a man for his strategy.'

I understood it was one of his metaphoric remarks, not meant to be unpacked. I caught his eye and dropped my own gaze, aware that I wasn't yet allowed to look people in the eye, especially not elders.

Dan spoke again: '*Ndifuna kanye undijonge.* Keep your head up, because I need you to look through me,' he told me. I heard the scandalised murmurs around us, as people took only the literal sense of his words. *Since when are initiates encouraged to look elders in the eye?* I could hear them thinking. But I read his words differently. It sounded to me as though he was saying: 'We have failed you in so many ways, *mfowam.* I therefore stand naked before you, surrendering myself to your scrutiny, so that you can see how much I regret what has befallen you.'

Rain peeled the blanket open so my head could come up and my eyes could meet *Oom* Dan's. I looked through them, as he had told me to, deep into his soul. The rest of the world was excluded from this moment; it was mine and Dan's alone. Our gazes locked for a long moment, and I thought I saw his soul weep.

And then Dan did something I couldn't believe, something that marked the beginning of true healing for the chest people. He turned the head of his knobkerrie around and handed it to me with both hands, reverently. I took it carefully, reluctantly, waiting for further instruction, not understanding why he was giving me his knobkerrie when he knew I already had my own. My confusion deepened when he turned away and went to assume his position without a further word.

Rain covered my head with the blanket again and silence fell in the kraal. No other man came to talk to me after Dan. There was an unusual stillness about everything. Slowly I realised the honour that had been conferred on me. What I held in my hands was more than just a knobkerrie; I'd been given the privilege to handle the manhood of a grown man.

23

I haven't seen Yanda again. My promised statement of symbols was delivered the same afternoon as I was preparing to leave the house of the lamp. I was busy cleaning up the yard, collecting bones and other carcasses to burn, when a white station wagon pulled up outside our gate. The driver annoyed me by hooting at me. I hated that; I wasn't a small boy to be hooted at any more. I thought perhaps it was one of Mother's colleagues, delivering a belated present for me. It turned out to be Yanda's cousin. He'd been requested by her to deliver my statement of symbols, plus the celebration present she'd promised me. With difficulty I resisted asking him about Yanda. Why had she not come in person? Where was she?

After he'd pulled away, I took the parcel to my room. Inside was an A4 envelope and a smart white *Dobs* hat, decorated with two guinea fowl feathers held on by a black band. I opened the envelope and retrieved two pieces of paper. One was my statement of symbols; the other, a short letter. I started with the statement of symbols, studying it closely and with pride. It turned out I'd got four Cs and three Ds, one of the Cs being for the extra subject I'd taken. I was satisfied with my results.

After that I read the note. It was written in point-form style – typical of Yanda. It didn't give me the answers I'd been hoping for.

Dear Chris,

I don't know where to begin. There is so much to say and yet the reason to do so no longer exists.

Maybe I should start by congratulating you on clinching university grades. I saw the statement, you did very well. I am proud. In fact, we are all proud of you, Chris. You should've seen V-Nesh and MC-Squared. They were so happy for you.

Can you believe it; la *way still wagged a finger at me when I requested your statement of symbols. This time I was tempted to ask her what the matter was. But you know how the head people always try to rationalise stuff. Anyway, whatever she was thinking, she was wrong.*

I hope you like the hat. It should fit you nicely if your head hasn't grown any bigger – kidding.

Please apologise on my behalf to sis *'Liz. I know I promised to deliver the statement in person.*

Anyway, take care of yourself. Maybe the next time I write, I will be telling you how everything has turned out while you were gone. Till next time.

Yanda

PS: I am sorry about your situation...

And that was that. It has now been more than seven years since I last saw or spoke to Yanda. I never did get to find out how everything turned out in her life. Or why she dumped me like she did. I still struggle to believe it was because of the way my circumcision went. She was the one person I could count on to understand things, and it still hurts to imagine that, in the end, she judged me like everyone else. If she wasn't willing to hear my side of the story, then who ever will be?

It is hard to explain the devastation I felt at having Yanda vanish so abruptly from my life. At first the pain was only emotional. It was more than just being abandoned by someone I loved; it was parting ways with a soul mate. A cruel thing, that.

Only later did I realise the dislocating effect her departure had on my life. My circumcision had come and gone. I'd achieved the university grades I'd worked so hard for. Okay, so now what? Where was Yanda with our Wits acceptance letters? I presumed she was not going to receive hers since she had not achieved a university pass. But what about mine? In her letter to me she had not mentioned anything about Wits, or suggested any other way forward for the two of us. The dream of our joint futures was shattered. The whole plan had come crashing down just like that.

That's the trouble with planning: it is not enough just to have a plan A. You have to have a B, too... even a C, all the way up to Z, if you like. This I unfortunately learnt after the fact. At the time I had no fall-back options at all. All I knew was that I wasn't going to stay at home and do nothing, like so many other matriculants. What would become of me if I remained in this village, this home? I didn't belong in either.

I knew I had to face my fear and move on somewhere. But where? I couldn't just rock up alone at Wits and say... my girlfriend applied for me... so what? I needed to go to a place I knew. And there was no place like that other than Cape Town. It was time to stare the monster in the eye. And this time, I was going to make it play by my rules. I was going to make *kasi* dance to my music, not the other way round.

Mother was talking about me going to one of those small colleges, Damelin, Boston, Varsity College, or whatever. But I wasn't interested. I had no intention of staying on in the Eastern Cape Province. The head people told me my healing wouldn't come from that place. Actually, it was one of the few times that the head people and chest people spoke with one voice.

As usual it turned out that I didn't need to argue with Mother. She didn't have a problem with me going back to Sodom and Gomorrah, as she now called Cape Town. Her only condition was that I should make peace with my father, speak to him like the adult I now was. She said I might as well put my university-level brains to the test while I was about it: intimidate my father with my matric education.

I didn't know if she was joking or not but it was a tempting thought. I could imagine my father's face when I told him: 'I am utterly flabbergasted that you still talk in the past tense, you know. I am no longer running amok and causing havoc like a headless chicken. I want us to move on to the simple present tense, you see.'

'I will leave the decisions to you, my son. You are not a child any more but a grown man. You can think for yourself now,' my mother said.

'The problem will be finding a place to stay,' I told her.

'My son, you still live a life of fears? After all that God has done for you? He stayed with you at the mountain when no one else was there, when I, your mother, couldn't even be there for you. You still doubt Him? How else should God show His love for you? You asked for a university pass and you got it. Hallelujah! Just tell me when you are planning to go and what you are looking for in Cape Town, and I will ask Him and He shall give us.'

And so it was that two weeks later I found myself at the bus station in Cape Town, waiting for *Ta'*Yongs to collect me. The DMJ bus had arrived a little earlier than scheduled. I sat there thinking my own thoughts in a roomful of strangers, some waiting for their relatives to come and pick them up, others waiting to board buses and depart to their destinations.

I was surprised by the fact that so many of these people were foreigners, mostly from elsewhere in Africa. They were speaking languages I didn't understand, and you could see from the tension in their faces that they weren't here to play. They were here to work, and no one works harder than our brothers and sisters from up north. There were bigger problems where they came from than the ones we faced, especially for the brothers and sisters from Congo and Somalia where the war is still ongoing. By comparison, our problems of endless protesting over service delivery appear like indulgences.

*Ta'*Yongs arrived eventually, wearing his brown prison warder uniform. He had come to pick me up in the GG, which was what he called the Department of Correctional Services Mazda 323 that he was driving. GG was what was written on the number plate. *Ta'*Yongs had been working at the notorious Pollsmoor prison for the past year but had been on compulsory leave for the whole of December, pending his transfer to one of the smaller prisons in the Western Cape. That's the reason he had been able to attend my circumcision. His bosses had been forced to relocate him after it had reached their ears that some of the other warders were conspiring with prisoners to have him murdered, after he'd blown the whistle on their drug smuggling business. *Ta'*Yongs had agreed to let me use his flat in Plumstead while he was gone and, in fact, was glad to have someone stay there and look after the place in his absence.

We drove into the southern suburbs of Cape Town. I felt strangely disorientated. The place looked different somehow from the last time I'd seen it. It didn't resemble the suburban goldmine I'd been digging into two years ago but looked more like a dead animal; so vulnerable, as if it had been brutalised just recently. This place that was once my own private mine, where I dug for gold and money, now resembled Sbenga's wounded dog. Or maybe it was me who was so broken, and not the poor suburbs.

*Ta'*Yongs delivered me to his flat and after we'd unloaded my things from the car, I helped him load his own luggage in.

'When one man arrives, the other must go,' he said jokingly.

'The difference is that you are the only man here,' I answered. It was the first time I'd felt comfortable referring to my situation. *Ta'*Yongs, if anyone, was a person with whom I could discuss it openly. He had been there through the difficult times of my circumcision, and he understood my situation through and through.

'What do you mean I'm the only man here? Are you saying

that all the time I sacrificed to attend your going-in ceremony, all the risk that Rain and I took on your behalf, subjecting our own manhood to scrutiny, all of that was a waste of time? If that is the case then... I have been lying to myself thinking that I know a man when I see one. And all those giant men who taught me what it is to be a man are also liars. Either that or you are a liar. You be the judge.'

There was silence.

'And just for the record, I won't leave my home in the care of a man who is not a man.'

What could I say to that? Tears choked the words in my throat. I pressed the remote and the electric gate slid open like a wound. The Mazda 323, otherwise known as GG, pulled out, and with a wave of its driver's hand, disappeared.

I stood there watching it go, while the wound I'd opened healed itself slowly, taking its own time.

After all, this was the time for the healing of wounds.

So now you have the story: I have a deformed penis. I'm a statistic and I'm a flawed man in the eyes of some. You can reach your own verdict on whether I'm a man or not when you've finished this story. But first, you may want to know how it all turned out.

I made my peace with Cape Town. I signed up for a Bachelor of Arts degree at UCT, from where I graduated with distinction. After that I spent a few sleepless nights trying to decide where the road went next. It took a while, but you'll be glad to hear I finally found my niche: working as a researcher for our national Broadcasting Corporation. That's right; I'm part of the *Simunye* team now. I've even got the T-shirt! In case you've ever wondered who it is that provides all that behind-the-scenes information for those news reports and exposés you watch, it's me.

As far as my limb is concerned, it's getting on nicely, thanks. The pinkness has disappeared and the colour has darkened to a nice manly shade of brown. Even better, it's slowly regaining its proper shape. To my great surprise the tissue of the head is growing back. S'true! My limb is slowly becoming its normal self again. I'm grateful for every hardness I wake up with. Even though it feels like punishment most of the time, I'm still happy that it's there. And one day I will put it to good use... so I keep promising myself.

Now that the head is growing back, the skewness of things

does not worry me as much. But in the beginning, when my limb still looked so tiny and sickly at the head, I admit I thought about seeking help to extend it. I'd collected a good variety of those leaflets that you get on street corners in town – you know the ones, offering help to make it longer and bigger. At one stage my junk mail at work had more than a hundred and fifty emails, all promising to make it bigger at affordable prices. Like I said, I did think about it but then decided no, I wasn't going to do it. I wasn't about to go for some artificial penis makeover.

A physical renovation on its own wouldn't have solved things, anyway. The damage that occurred and the subsequent scars that developed were not only physical, see. There was a mental and emotional train smash that happened simultaneously, and that was the more serious worry. Writing about it here, letting you know what really happened, is like using the Jaws of Life to save a soul that has been crushed under the wreckage of sorrow.

My grandfather and I still haven't spoken about it. When I go home to visit, we greet each other and talk about the weather. That's the limit of our conversation. I am still waiting for a word of apology from him, though he has made some gestures that imply guilt and regret in his thoughts. The other morning, for instance, I found him at the kraal, working on some leather thing with a stone.

'Morning, Grandfather,' I greeted him, expecting the usual cursory exchange and nothing more than that.

'Morning, *mfo*,' he replied. There was silence.

Then he retrieved the rest of the goatskin from under his stool and I saw what he was preparing. He was making a leather thong for my younger brother, who is due for circumcision at the end of this coming year.

'The boy has advanced,' Grandfather said. He turned the leather over for me to see the side that was done. 'We need to be prepared.'

At that moment I realised that my grandfather was initiating a man's conversation with me for the first time. But I need more from him. I'm waiting for him to say something about me, my manhood, and the "failure" of it. To come out with it directly in the same blunt way that he never minced his words when he accused me of being fragile. Only then can I say to him what I need to. It is for him to raise the subject, not me. The head people are stubborn as hell. They would rather break the taboo of silence and proclaim my situation to the whole world, so that it does not poison my system any further, than initiate a discussion about it with Grandfather.

Writing about what happened is the only way I can say what I have to say and put it behind me. It isn't possible to discuss these things at home. The subject is avoided; it just got buried and has stayed buried for over seven years, never mentioned by anyone. My own family treat me with caution. To this day, Mother and Grandmother still don't know the real story of what happened to me. They don't know if I even have a penis. They hear the stories of what goes on in hospital, of men urinating through pipes, and they wonder if that's what happened to me. But women can't ask, like; what happens at the mountain stays at the mountain.

I still have a few outstanding questions of my own. What about being with a woman, you know? What will she think? What will she say when she sees my limb that is still busy growing itself back to what it was? How will I explain my differently shaped manhood to her? I haven't yet had the courage to test that one out. I am caught between the worry over my physical appearance and my need to finally part ways with my goddamn innocence. Yes, that is still in the pipeline, like.

My good looks and politeness don't help anything. Whether it's at work, university or shopping malls, hot babes fall over their feet when they see me. All my friendships with women tend to end dramatically, though. Because I don't take them to bed, they end up hating me for it. They might not say so, but I can see them thinking that I must be gay. And my fluid, urban taste does not help anything, either. But I know that one day it will happen. And when it does, you are gonna read about it!

My relationships with other men, particularly Xhosa men, tend to be superficial. I have mastered the three-part handshake, the salutations and other basics. I can also talk the talk – apologies for the cliché – and leave it at that. I don't allow them to come too close because then a discussion about manhood is inevitable. It's not so much fear of being found out that makes me avoid the subject these days, but because I know that in the heads of my opponents, such a debate is already won. As a supposedly failed man, my opinion doesn't matter, irrespective of its merit. There's no point in talking about such things to someone who is not listening.

What's ironic is that I don't discuss these things with *amakrwala*, new men, either. Not even those that I have visited at the huts during their seclusion and taught what I know about manhood. By the time they get to the house of the lamp, they know everything there is to know about being a man – thanks to my instruction. I help to make men. But when their initiation is over and they're being welcomed as real men, I see in their eyes how confused they are that I, who have taught them so much, should be called a bogus man. Yet these things, we never talk about. I wish they would ask me, because that would give me the opening to talk freely with them about my own experiences.

These days I'm more comfortable with men of other tribes than my own. This type, I let into my space freely. Our discussions about manhood begin on a levelled premise: that we're all of us "not men" as prescribed by my particular culture. We debate cross-culturally, without the limitations or coded exchanges meant to prove that some are less manly than others. These talks are fruitful all round.

But all of this has made me lead a split life for far too long. I've had to learn to be a real man among real men, while being an ordinary man among ordinary men.

Oh, the energy it takes to live the life of a split man! Constantly having to defend myself through silence for my unique path into manhood.

Sometimes, when the frustration of having no voice, no space to be a man in my own right, grows too much for the head people, I feel my manhood shrinking. I feel it curl to the side like an earthworm. That is why I decided – shit! I'm letting the story out to make myself heard and claim my space as a man once and for all.

It's also a way of cheating those bastards who've been volunteering uncalled-for tales about my fall. Gotcha, you rumour-mongers! You've been going around gossiping about me in dark corners, and I admit I have been bothered about it. Well, I've made your job easier by writing this, don't you think? You've got it now from the horse's mouth – apologies for another cliché.

Actually, I'm not half as bothered by the gossip as I used to be. Strangely enough, my supposedly "failed" circumcision has made me feel more like a real man, not less. If manhood is about enduring pain in its figurative and literal sense, then I dare say I have more than earned it. I understand now what *Oom* Dan meant when he said: '*Ubudoda licebo.*' A man is a man for his strategy.

The question I ask myself is: If I had to undergo the same process with the same result, would I make the same decisions? Given what I know now – my penis losing its cosmetic value, me being gossiped about and vilified, even ostracised from humanity, at least in the eyes of my community – would I adopt the same strategy? Would I still turn myself in at the hospital like I did? I have hated and received as much hatred. I have felt the electrocution of loneliness and been labelled a non-human. Given all that, would I still choose the House of

Ruin over death on the mountain? Who in their right mind would say 'Yes'?

Well I got news for you: ME. I'm the fool who would do it all over again. I mean, wouldn't you also choose to repeat the unique journey that helped you find your clarity and true manhood?

I've come to realise that far from having failed as a man, my experience has allowed me a deeper understanding of what manhood is really about. It has made me more of a human, not less. Who I have become is exactly who I am meant to be. Other men may continue to judge me, but their opinion no longer matters. Just as in seclusion a man must heal himself without dependency on others, so the same is true of the journey of life.

And so ends the sermon about my abnormal penis.

Transforming a manuscript into the book you are now reading is a team effort. Cassava Republic Press would like to thank everyone who helped in the production of *A Man Who Is Not A Man*:

Editorial
Bibi Bakare-Yusuf
Layla Mohamed

Design & Production
AI's Fingers

Sales & Marketing
Kofo Okunola
Lynette Lisk

Support *A Man Who Is Not a Man*

We hope you enjoyed reading this book. It was brought to you by Cassava Republic Press, an award-winning independent publisher based in Abuja and London. If you think more people should read this book, here's how you can support:

1. **Recommend it.** Don't keep the enjoyment of this book to yourself; tell everyone you know. Spread the word to your friends and family.
2. **Review, review review**. Your opinion is powerful and a positive review from you can generate new sales. Spare a minute to leave a short review on Amazon, GoodReads, Wordery, our website and other book buying sites.
3. **Join the conversation.** Hearing somebody you trust talk about a book with passion and excitement is one of the most powerful ways to get people to engage with it. If you like this book, talk about it, Facebook it, Tweet it, Blog it, Instagram it. Take pictures of the book and quote or highlight from your favourite passage. You could even add a link so others know where to purchase the book from.
4. **Buy the book as gifts for others.** Buying a gift is a regular activity for most of us – birthdays, anniversaries, holidays, special days or just a nice present for a loved one for no reason... If you love this book and you think it might resonate with others, then please buy extra copies!
5. **Get your local bookshop or library to stock it.** Sometimes bookshops and libraries only order books that they have heard about. If you loved this book, why not ask your librarian or bookshop to order it in. If enough people request a title, the bookshop or library will take note and will order a few copies for their shelves.
6. **Recommend a book to your book club.** Persuade your book club to read this book and discuss what you enjoy about the book in the company of others. This is a wonderful way to share what you like and help to boost the sales and popularity of this book. You can also join our online book club on Facebook at Afri-Lit Club to discuss books by other African writers.
7. **Attend a book reading.** There are lots of opportunities to hear writers talk about their work. Support them by attending their book events. Get your friends, colleagues and families to a reading and show an author your support.

Thank you!

Stay up to date with the latest books, special offers and exclusive content with our monthly newsletter.

Sign up on our website:
www.cassavarepublic.biz

#AManWho #ReadCassava #ReadingAfrica
Twitter: @cassavarepublic | Instagram: @cassavarepublicpress
Facebook: facebook.com/CassavaRepublic